Pushing Pawns

The Chess Club Book One

DIMA NOVAK

The characters and events portrayed in this book are fictitious. Any similarity to real persons, living or dead, is coincidental and not intended by the author.

ISBN: 9798494351074

Printed in the United States of America

DEDICATION

To Molly, my romance heroine.

CONTENTS

I don't enjoy being a Minister. I would rather play chess, or make a revolution in Venezuela.

1. LOSING

"Checkmate."

The blond kid with the IZOD sweater smirked as he waved his delicate pink hand over the board, offering to shake.

"Better luck next time," he added, twisting the knife.

Scholar's mate. The oldest trick in the book. Four quick moves and you're a dead baby joke. Worst part was, I knew how to counter it — had known since I was a little kid — but he'd gotten inside my head with his floppy rich-boy haircut and his black leather chess bag. They call it chess blindness. I was thinking three or four moves ahead, designing a devastating attack, when my brain shorted out. Played Nf6, flatlined.

Every patzer in the storied NYC Chess in the Schools program knows that trap, and the fact that he tried it on me at all was pure disrespect, a way of showing his contempt. Contempt for my neighborhood, my skills, my school. Contempt for me: Moses Middleton, freshman, fresh kid, and all-round mediocrity at Q722, the Phillips Exeter of northern Queens (joke).

Contempt, derision, scorn, and about a million other SAT vocab words that I'm going to need to get into a decent college — and which will probably be useful in the meantime for describing the humiliation I experience every day. Chess was supposed to be a way to make my mark at school, to stand out from the nobodies who get shoulder-checked in the hallways and trashed on social media. Instead, I'd been posterized. I sucked, and the proof was right there on the tournament scoreboard.

I slunk out of the cafeteria and slipped outside the school building to blow a cloud or three, palming my trusty mini-mod. I wasn't alone. Dimly visible in the shadow of the school dumpster was my classmate P.D. Morales, wild-haired and olive-skinned, looking like Teenage Satan behind a swirling mist of vaporized Unicorn Milk. We bumped and commenced lurking.

"You rolled over for Barron Trump I hear. Nice. I am already composing snarky tweets in my head." He exhaled a monumental cloud. "Can't help it: they come to me unbidden."

P.D., undoubtedly the smartest kid in Q722, was a social pariah and a spectacular academic failure, majoring in underachievement with a minor in truancy. Nobody messed with him, though. The consequences were too dire. Supposedly in Middle School he'd bitten off a sizeable chunk of a classmate's earlobe. The nickname stood for Personality Disorder.

"Thanks a lot, problem child," I replied. "So what are you doing out here so soon? Round's hardly started."

"As you would know, loser. It happens that I drew one of those Galton Prep kids, just like you did. I figured I'd let 20 or 25 minutes run off the clock. Once he's sure he has the game in the bag, I'm going back in and steamroller his sorry ass. Can't wait to see him crumble. I give it three minutes."

"Speaking of which ...." He glanced at his vintage Casio — a coveted classic, the one with Space Invaders pre-installed — and pocketed his mod. "It's time to explode some smug preppy's class prejudices. See you on the obverse side."

P.D. was some kind of bona fide chess genius, and probably the New York City leader in disqualifications. He never studied, preferred to go online and play twisted chess variants like crazyhouse and atomic. Sometimes he could be persuaded to join the team for a random tournament, spotting us an automatic four points — provided he didn't throw a tantrum and sweep someone's pieces off the board, or just drift away and disappear in the middle of a match.

Me? I was "promising." Or so I was told one day when I dropped into the Queens Chess Academy on a whim and played skittles with the coach, a woman grandmaster with a heavy accent and a global reputation. (The awesome thing about chess in New York is that *anybody* will give you a game, anywhere, anytime.)

Possibly because of my ambiguous skin color, I got a vibe that she expected me to play street chess — you know: all tactics, no strategy; traps, diversions, kamikaze queen attacks, that kind of crap. So when I played a meticulous Caro-Kann instead (*boring!*), she nodded her approval ... before wiping me out. I never signed up for lessons (too expensive), but her praise, and the chess-mad atmosphere of the place, was an inspiration. I volunteered to organize a chess club at school; first time I'd ever volunteered for anything. Managed to recruit a handful of classmates, leveraging the unexpected coolness that attached to the game after that TV show featuring the sexy, drug-addled chess genius.

Meanwhile, I began to study some on my own, learning openings from books and trying them out with 10-minute games online. Sometimes I'd hit the chess tables at Travers Park, where a motley crew of homeless dudes and hustlers sat around waiting for a mark. One of them, an old Russian guy named Viktor, was rumored to be an international grandmaster who'd lost his marbles and run out of luck. I had never quite worked up the nerve to challenge him but promised myself I would, someday.

Eventually I got savvy enough to out-think a lot of high school players. But it never came easy for me. Only once or twice have I experienced any part of The Zone – that trippy *Black Mirror* place where the chess board is the universe, where everything's unconscious instinct and non-Euclidean geometry. Like what the TV chess babe sees on her ceiling after popping her pills.

P.D., like his hero Magnus Carlsen, *lives* in The Zone. Me, I'm stuck right here in Jackson Heights, Queens.

By the time I made it back to the cafeteria, the scorer was already recording P.D.'s victory, while his nattily attired opponent was staring at the final position, heels up and gasping. The stragglers were rolling up their boards and heading for the snack machine.

I checked the standings on the whiteboard. Q722 was 1-3, good for last place, while the fetal stockbroker squad from Galton was 3-1, leading the pack. Damn. Dead in the water. If I hadn't messed up, we might still be in the mix, or at least we could have been somewhere north of the cellar.

I sighed, taking in a deep lungful of that unmistakable cafeteria aroma: sour milk, stale apples, a hint of dirty sneaker. Shaking off my shame, I ambled over to greet my fellow losers at our table in the corner. Maggie was, as usual after a loss, sniffling quietly, her delicate features screwed up into a mask of tragedy behind a pair of big ugly nerd glasses. She was super sensitive. Surprising myself, I felt a sharp pang of sympathy, but I had to suppress an impulse to offer comfort: Not only would it be uncool, but worse, it would look like I was creeping her.

No chance of that with my other teammate, Esther, who would've kicked my ass at the first hint of commiseration; she just looked mad. And mean. She rolled her eyes and put on her best English accent, as absorbed from countless BBC period romances. I called it "Austening." Sometimes she would roll out an actual Jane Austen quote; sometimes it was just an improvisation in high-flown Britspeak.

"Thanks to your egregious performance, Moses, I surmise that we can look forward to yet another Saturday afternoon of pointless endeavor," she Austened.

Making a mental note of the vocab, I did my best to respond in kind.

"I beg you to expect my humblest apologies, milady, but I feel compelled to point out that you, too, experienced a crushing defeat."

"Right, Mose, but you're the one who's supposed to be taking this seriously." Back to her normal voice, best described as Token Minority Newscaster with a slight overlay of Haitian Creole. "I'm just here to hang with Maggie. I guess *you're* here to carry water for White Privilege Academy."

Whoa. She shot me the The Look and returned to whatever she was doing on her phone. Esther was an intimidating presence, tall, jet-black, and muscly, like those apparently superhuman physical specimens you see competing in Olympic track and field. She was, however, not a runner but a fencer. Not that she gave much of a damn about athletics – for her, it was all about music; everything else took a back seat to her precious violin.

"Very cold, Esther. Glacial. I'm humiliated enough as it is. Besides, didn't you notice that Galton's third board is a Black kid?"

"At Galton, *fam,"* — she gave the word withering emphasis — "even the black kids are white. Walking ads for *diversity and inclusion.* They started their LinkedIn pages when they were in kindergarten. They 'curate' blogs to build their personal brands. They run their own NGOs. Yale's admissions office is already salivating."

"You're one to talk, Black Mozart." (There's a story behind that; I'll get to it later.) "Playing chamber music in the public library isn't exactly what you'd call keeping it real."

"Doesn't matter, Mose." Suddenly serious. "My skin is, like, purple. I'm styling a no-brand hoodie with tatty tights from the discount store on 82nd Street. Single-parent household. Rice and beans for dinner. I don't see myself in an eating club at Princeton, and no one else will either. SUNY-bound, if I'm lucky. I'm Q722 through and through. You know our motto: 'So diverse it's perverse.'"

I looked over at Maggie, who seemed to be done crying and was sliding a textbook out of her backpack. Caught her eye; desperately tried to think of something to say.

"Um, well, we're all 0-1 except P.D., so at least we'll be paired with patzers in the next round," I stammered. "Good chance to steal a win."

She nodded gravely and cracked open *Intermediate French.* So much for that conversational gambit. I won't lie: I was seriously attracted to Maggie, pathological shyness, bad glasses, and all. I was kind of into Esther too. To be honest, I was half in love with pretty much any girl who'd talk to me. But Maggie, well, Maggie was special.

I heard an echoing rush of sneakered feet as the second-round pairings were posted at the scorer's table, saving me from further awkwardness. I drew a guy I'd never heard of from Newtown High – a kid so obviously nerdy that he made me look gangsta by comparison – and somehow I knew I owned his ass from the moment I started the clock. He tried to play the Sicilian but didn't seem to know the opening beyond the first couple of moves. I took control of the center, grabbed a bishop after a blunder, and then methodically traded down to an endgame that was a foregone conclusion. He did us both a favor and resigned.

Maggie and Esther won their games, too, while for P.D., who was facing a much stronger opponent this time, it took a full five minutes to force a checkmate. Suddenly we were 5-3, and things didn't look quite so grim for Q722. Hell, I was beginning to feel a little optimistic.

Then Round Three hit us. Like a hypersonic missile. I drew a Russian kid from Elmhurst, played the Four Knights, found myself in a slow agonizing grind, always on the defensive, extricating myself from one complex positional nightmare after another. At last he offered a trade; I accepted gratefully. The dam burst. A dizzying cascade of exchanges left me a pawn down in the endgame. Didn't have the heart to play it out. Another big L.

P.D., needless to say, made short work of some arrogant little hotshot who came equipped with his own chess clock. But the girls both lost, so we finished the round at six and six, far from disgraced but definitely out of the running.

Now came the low point of any tournament, the part where you need to slog through one more game when there's no longer anything to play for. It's getting late, you're starting to get hungry, you feel the weekend slipping away from you. All you want to do is put it in the books and go home. The only thing left to look forward to was P.D.'s game. He'd be matched against some other kid with three points; barring a draw — and P.D. *never* drew — the winner would be taking home the individual trophy, a huge plastic monstrosity that could work as a lawn ornament, if any of us had lawns.

I was matched with a girl from Garden School, big and Irish-looking with a bad case of the sniffles. I guess that was her secret weapon. Waiting for her next gurgling gasp, knowing it was coming but not knowing when, was like Chinese water torture. Distracting as hell. Still I managed to stay focused enough to eke out a win. Out of stubbornness or spite, maybe just hoping for the stalemate, she refused to resign and I had to checkmate her with rook and king. Took forever.

I cruised over to the scorer's table for the results. Maggie won; Esther lost. But it was a kind of a shock seeing the "L" next to P.D.'s name. WTF? He'd been paired with Galton's best player; he would've relished taking the guy apart.

Maggie materialized at my shoulder and gravely told me the news.

"P.D. was disqualified again. He did one of his disappearing acts. Never showed up for Round Four."

Furious but not entirely surprised, I dropped an F-bomb that echoed in the halls, then quickly blurted an apology. Maggie hated swearing.

Esther joined us, shrugging on her jacket. She glanced at the scoreboard and rolled her eyes.

"Typical. We finish at .500, perfectly mediocre. And Galton kicked our ass again. Forgive me if I don't stay for the awards ceremony." She sighed theatrically. "Another Saturday wasted."

Well, I was hurt, and more than a little pissed off – which led me to say exactly the wrong thing.

"Hey, friend, nobody forced you to play. We chilled, played a few games, added something to the résumé. It's not like you had anything better to do."

Esther's eyes flashed.

"You serious? I could've gone running. I could've been practicing scales. I could've been watching romcoms on Netflix. Hell, I could've been lying on my bed, smoking weed and staring out the window. Just about anything would've been better than spending all day in the school lunchroom with a bunch of chronic masturbators and acne casualties."

I was speechless. Maggie threw me a bone. "Well, *I* enjoyed it very much, and I'm sure Mose did, too."

"Girl, you were in tears half the time!" Esther snapped. "And the other half, you were studying French. Sometimes I think you just *pretend* to like these tournaments so you can drag me along and keep me out of trouble."

Maggie looked stricken. "But I *like* chess." After a pause, in a voice so quiet that it might as well have been a whisper: "And it's better than being at home."

That freaked me out a little bit, and I realized I knew nothing at all about Maggie's home life. None of my business, I thought. Looking back on it now, I feel like a selfish dickhead, but right then I was too obsessed with my own bullshit to worry about anyone else, even the girl I liked most.

Maggie, whose Chinese first name was Meiling, had been friend-zoning me since Middle School, where we shared a lab bench in Physical Science class. Right away, 13-year-old me had feelings for her, and it was more than just hormones. I couldn't even have told you why. She was painfully shy; I was awkward as hell — still am, I guess — and I tried to break the ice in a million ways, primarily dumb jokes. Nothing worked.

So I fished for shared interests. In high school you can begin to sort other kids out in the same way adults label people, by what they *do*: this one's a basketball player, that one's a Siemens scholar, this one's a hardened criminal, and so on. In Middle School, kids' identities haven't really jelled, so you try to figure them out not by what they do, but what they *like*. At first there didn't seem to be any common ground. She read poetry. Not my thing. She was into fanart — her notebooks were elaborately decorated with pencil sketches of Goku and various googly-eyed princesses — but I was not the *otaku* type. Although I loved certain genres of corny old movies, anime left me cold.

Then one day I happened to bring my chess bag to class and hit the jackpot. Turned out Maggie was a secret chess fiend. We exchanged our online chess handles and played a shedload of games after hours, bantering in the chat box. It didn't lead to any kind of romance but at least we made a connection. For a while. Since high school started, I rarely found Maggie online, and as for real life, she and Esther were now besties and stuck together like Pritt. I saw her almost exclusively at club meetings and tournaments. No chess, no Maggie.

So I was shook when Esther turned to me as we were leaving and spoke confidentially, out of Maggie's hearing.

"Face it, Mose. The little chess club you organized is imploding. If Maggie wants to play, I guess I'll support her for a while. But I'm thinking it's time to accept that we're all mediocrities and go our separate ways."

I deflated like yesterday's birthday balloon. Maybe she was right. I'd put my heart and soul into organizing the club, but I'd probably do myself a favor by focusing more on academics and – *puke* – résumé-building. And I wouldn't have to ride herd on a small group of outsize personalities with problems even bigger than mine. Apart from the opportunity to see Maggie, why did I bother?

Outside the school, we saw the kids from Galton. Laughing, shoulder-punching, scrambling into a G-Class SUV. Cruising into a future of guaranteed success with sweaters draped elegantly around their shoulders. Rolling back to their tastefully appointed apartments where they'd be congratulated by their prosperous, coolly affectionate parents. None of them spared us a glance. I realized that we were invisible to the Galton kids, like the service workers who supported their friction-free lifestyles.

Me, I was invisible to everybody — except when I wasn't. Turned out, my already horrendous day was about to get worse.

I shrugged on my hoodie, stuffed my hands in my pockets, and motored homewards. To get there, I needed to slide through the schmancy quarter. The Jackson Heights Historic District was an oasis of green gardens and pre-war brick row houses, maybe the prettiest neighborhood in Queens. As my dad once explained to me, JH was a planned community built in the1920s under what they called a restrictive covenant — meaning no Blacks; no Jews; wypipo only. Things loosened up after the war when openly racist contracts were struck down by the courts, and for a while even the Historic District was getting pretty diverse. Now, though, pale-faced gentrifiers were returning to the area in force, swaggering down the street toting Osprey backpacks and little plastic bags of dogshit, trailing high-priced coffee shops and artisanal liquor stores in their wake. Suddenly the homes were too expensive for regular families. These days I never felt comfortable in the territory of the young professionals and "knowledge workers." I only relaxed once I crossed the border, Roosevelt Avenue, where real people from places like Bangladesh and Colombia did business under the roaring, shuddering tracks of the elevated train.

I was still traversing the yuppie beachhead when I stopped by a bodega to grab a Coke. I found myself in line just behind a Jackson Heights hipster, a perfect specimen of the rude-ass interlopers who were now my neighbors. A big soft guy in cargo shorts with a shaggy blond beard and — get this — a fanny pack. (Why TF would you wear a fanny pack when you've got, like, 15 pockets in your pants?) The man was planting his feet and striking a pose, hands on hips, obviously getting set to create some drama.

"What do you mean, you don't support Apple Pay?" He was actually ridiculing the clerk's accent (*you dawn soppor' Opple Pay*). Then, in his own adenoidal voice, he delivered a lecture, over-enunciating every word like he assumed the guy couldn't understand English. He pulled his iPhone out, waving it around as he spoke.

"You *need* to support Apple Pay. If you want my business, *bro*, you'd better update your attitude and join the 21st Century."

The clerk, who was probably well used to this kind of bullshit, calmly told him the business was cash-only. Whereupon the yuppie dude slammed his canned smoothie down on the counter and flounced out of the store, shouting "*Eff* you, man!" over his shoulder. (I'm going to try to avoid spelling out the eff-word in this, my magnum opus, but of course you know which swear is intended.)

Guys like him were everywhere these days, fuming at anyone who failed to defer to their whims. An occupying army of whining babies, scoring points in their own infantile video game: *Call of Doody*. I made sympathetic eye contact with the clerk as I paid for my soda.

I paused on the corner to check for texts. It was dark by now; my mom might be ringing in for a status check. Out of nowhere — *wham!* — I felt a smack on my shoulder, hard enough that I stumbled forward a couple of steps. I wheeled around and saw the hipster from the bodega, goggle-eyed and breathing hard; he was *rage*.

"You effing little *shit*! Give me my effing *phone*!" he yelled, his voice cracking. He threw up his little fists and actually executed an awkward bounce step, looking ridiculous and scary at the same time. Things were about to go critical.

I was briefly paralyzed with shock, which was probably a good thing. If I'd taken a defensive stance, some kind of fist fight was going to happen. Not that I couldn't have taken this guy — well, okay, he had like 60 pounds on me so maybe not — but a street altercation was bound to attract the cops. And like my dad always warns me, I need to avoid *any* kind of interaction with NYPD. A brown kid in a hoodie is automatically the Bad Guy. Doesn't matter if I'm the injured party; doesn't matter if I've just discovered the cure for cancer. I could end up cuffed. Or tased. Or worse. So, hating myself, I just backed away, slowly.

"I don't have your phone, man," I said, as calmly as I could. "No idea what you're talking about."

He advanced, spluttering. "You were right next to me in the store. My phone is gone. I can see it right there in your dirty little hand. Give it back — *now!* — or I'm calling the police."

Dirty little hand. He was *that* close to spitting out the N-word; you can always tell. I was dazed and furious, overcome by conflicting emotions. I thought about running, but that would seem like an admission of guilt. The whole messed-up situation teetered on the knife-edge; I experienced a massive shot of adrenalin and it felt like the world snapped into sharp focus. Suddenly I could hear the background noise — indistinct voices, a barking dog, the rumble of traffic — in hi-res audio. It was like the movies: a beat of tension music; a fateful pause; an explosion of chaotic violence.

Then, thankfully, the cavalry rode in. The electronic chime on the bodega door sounded, and the clerk emerged with an iPhone in his hand.

"I think you left your phone, boss," he deadpanned. I thought I detected an ironic stress on the word "boss," but it was hard to be sure. He kept a perfectly straight face. Like me, this was a man who had to watch his step all the time.

The hipster snatched his phone back. No word of thanks to the clerk. And for me, no apology whatsoever, even though he'd literally assaulted me. Far from it: He was going to save face by blaming the situation on me.

"Maybe you shouldn't be lurking on the corner in your hoodie, homes. You're on *my* turf. You'd best be watching your back."

I'd seen this before. People like him thought of themselves as the neighborhood aristocracy. They could never admit to being wrong, especially in front of the peasants. Ironically, I had absolutely no doubt that he was the type to attend rallies for justice, shouting woke slogans and calling out "systemic racism." Probably had a closet full of BLM T-shirts. I bet he even has a couple of special friends "of color" that he invites to the coffee shop to massage his ego and make him feel righteous.

Here was my opportunity to call him out, to recapture my dignity, but I was still too freaked out to think of a cutting remark. He waddled off triumphantly toward the Historic Preservation District, his fanny pack swaying. He'd straight-up profiled me, but my silence would allow him to keep thinking of himself as a paragon of Wokeness.

Was this going to be my life? Swallowing humiliation in order to save my skin? Doing a perpetual model minority act, just so I could land a job in some firm where I'd be reporting to snide hipsters like him, or worse, Galton's Masters of the Universe?

I brooded all the way home. Winning came so easy to all these bastards. The private school chess dilettantes, the imperial occupiers of my neighborhood, the smug CEO types who sometimes showed up at assemblies to lecture us about success.

No, I thought: This will not stand. Maybe I was channeling Lebowski, but the feeling was real, and very deep. I could do something to recapture my dignity. Maybe, just once, I could give those preening power jocks a taste of defeat. If not on the street, then over the board.

2. UNMIXED RACE

Sunday morning. I woke up from a weird chess dream, something about black and white armies trudging toward certain death across a checkered plain. It took a couple of seconds to realize there was no school today; mad relief. Then I remembered the previous day and instantly grimmed out.

As always in the morning, the first thing that met my eyes was the framed *Time Magazine* cover that my dad had hung on the wall over my dresser. A painted portrait of Roy Campanella, surrounded by a bunch of mitts, bats, balls, and hands frozen in motion, dated August 8, 1955. It was a joke gift that was actually kind of serious.

"Yo, Roy," I muttered as I ambled over to the bathroom to — as P.D. would say — shake hands with the unemployed.

Most kids my age don't remember Roy Campanella unless they're baseball obsessives (like I am), but he was Jackie Robinson's teammate on the Brooklyn Dodgers. In his time Campanella was the greatest catcher in baseball — maybe barring Yogi Berra, backstop of what my dad calls the "perpetually detestable Yankees." (We're all Mets fans; Citifield is like four subway stops away.) He'd given me the magazine to make sure I would never forget one of his patented Geek Dad Life Lessons.

Here's what happened. Over the dinner table a couple of years ago I'd told my parents about a lesson on racism I'd had in Middle School. The teacher, who was a pretty nice lady and meant well, asked the class for a show of hands.

"Who here is African-American? Who is white? Who is Hispanic?"

Then came my turn, or so I thought.

"Who is biracial?" I had thrown up my hand.

On hearing this, my dad's nostrils flared ever so slightly: He's a pretty mild-mannered guy, and I knew this meant he was seriously pissed off.

"Moses," he began quietly. "You're not 'biracial.' No one is 'biracial.' That word implies that we can identify and define two distinct races among human beings. If you'll pardon the expression, that's bullshit."

Mom sighed, preparing herself for the lecture to come. "Albert, can't we just have a quiet dinner?"

"When did we ever?" I snarked.

But there was no stopping him. "This is important. He's going to have to reckon with this kind of nonsense all his life."

"I would like to hear him out, Rose," said Mallika in an apologetic tone. She wanted my mom to understand that she was legit interested, not taking sides in a family dispute. Her husband, Ritwik, nodded in agreement.

I should clue you in about our dinner table. We're not your traditional mommy-daddy-me kind of family; we're more of an ongoing sitcom with a rotating cast. When I was just a toddler, Mom and Dad bought a big, run-down postwar house in Elmhurst, just across the line from gentrified Jackson Heights. Some absentee landlord had it set up as an informal, and probably illegal, Single Room Occupancy joint; it came cheap, but it was way too big for a three-person family.

So my parents, Albert and Rose, started renting out space, legally, to help with the mortgage. Over the years I've lived through a series of tangled but always entertaining story arcs — including dramas, comedies, and romances (no horror … yet) — as tenants moved in and out of our house and our lives. We've had graduate students, Fed Ex drivers, artists, wives on the run from abusive husbands, families newly arrived from Bangladesh or Guatemala who needed a transitional place to stay. We didn't advertise; it was all word-of-mouth.

Everyone said my parents were the best landlords they'd ever had. They were understanding about the rent, maybe to a fault, and were open to substituting barter for cash. Some of our tenants liked to cook, so we started having big, hippie-style communal dinners where everybody pitched in. The food was great; we all saved money; loud, lively arguments at the table were the norm.

Mallika was a law student and volunteered at a Legal Aid clinic; Ritwik was a resident at Elmhurst General Hospital. Their hours were crazy, so we didn't see them together all that often, but for once they were both free and had cooked an enormous meal of curried chicken and rice. Also present on that evening, if I remember right, were Dante, a Guatemalan guitarist who worked in a local restaurant, and Julian, a bearded, soft-spoken sculptor who reminded me of the beatnik dude in *Iron Giant.*

Now certain of his audience, Dad turned to me. "Mose, here's some baseball trivia. Which Italian-American player for the Brooklyn Dodgers once hit 40 home runs?"

I racked my brains.

"Carl Furillo?" I guessed, knowing I was wrong but figuring it couldn't hurt to play along. "Only Italian Dodger I can think of, off the top of my head."

"Nope, not even close. It was Roy Campanella."

"C'mon Dad, Campanella was Black!"

"Roy Campanella had a Sicilian-American father and an African-American mother. It's just as valid to think of him as Italian-American as it is to think of him as Black. We honor him as an African-American hero, not because of his DNA, but because he was *socially defined* as Black and had to negotiate the consequences. There's no such thing as race, not in a biological sense."

"Maybe there isn't any race, Dad, but there's color," I objected. "And it matters. It sure as hell affects the way people are treated in the US."

"And not just in the US," Mallika added. "In India light skin privilege is a serious issue. It's a global problem, and you cannot simply gloss over it."

"No doubt about it," Dad responded. "I experience it every day." Dad is a research biologist, a dark-skinned Ph.D. who wears a tie and talks like a university professor. He's the least scary-looking Black man you could imagine, but he gets hassled by cops and micro-aggressed by store clerks on a regular basis.

"But my skin color doesn't mean I belong to a particular 'race.' Brown skin just gives society an excuse to make assumptions about me based on an imaginary biological category. And it gives the powerful a way of dividing the rest of us from each other. To put it bluntly, the idea of 'race' was invented by our masters to justify crimes they were already committing."

Julian, who was usually way too chill to get involved in a dinner table debate, suddenly looked interested.

"Al, put you and me side-by-side in a line-up, people are going to see a *big* difference."

"Skin and hair, right?" my dad responded. "Really just skin. You're kind of olive-skinned, but your hair is almost as kinky as mine. Anyhow, skin and hair type are superficial differences, completely inconsequential from a biological point of view."

Needless to say, I was on full Vocab Alert.

"The fact is, you and I are both descendants of Africans who migrated to Europe, maybe as recently as 50,000 years ago," he continued. "That's an eyeblink. There wasn't enough time for humans to differentiate except in the most trivial ways – like skin color. There's probably more genetic similarity between the two of us than there is between a typical East African and a typical West African."

"Mind blown," Julian said. "Well and truly blown."

"People think it's woke to call someone like Moses 'biracial,' but all they're doing is finding a new category to force him into. Same with 'mixed race.' They're implying that there's a Race One and a Race Two, and when you mix them together you get Race Three. They don't even realize it, but they're just reviving old-fashioned, poisonous ideas about bloodlines. People start thinking of everything in terms of race, pretty soon we're talking eugenics."

My dad used to work at Cold Spring Harbor, a research lab in Long Island, where a few decades ago they used to cook up programs aimed at "improving the racial stock," mostly through scary stuff like selective breeding and sterilization. They called it eugenics, and Dad had super-sensitive radar where that was concerned.

Mom jumped in. "Albert, Mose's teacher just wants the kids to be comfortable with their identities. What's wrong with that?"

"Nothing, except that identity isn't the same as race. Brings me back to Roy Campanella: Mose is just as much entitled to identify as Jewish as he is to identify as Black. His identity isn't one thing, or two things: It's a complex and changing mixture of cultural heritage, language, geography, individual interests and proclivities, like his weird taste in movies (*more about that later*), his sexual orientation (*cringe!*), et cetera. I could go on, but I don't have to, right?"

"A gorgeous mosaic," Dante added, shooting mom and dad a wink. (Later I found out that he was quoting a New York City mayor from back in the day — a mayor that my parents actually *liked*.)

"Well, I hope that brings tonight's sermon to a close," I said. "Because I hate being discussed in the third person when I'm sitting right here. Plus I'm ready for dessert."

A few days later my dad gave me the Campanella mag, which he must have found on eBay, together with a little note saying: "Remember." Kind of passive-aggressive, but that's the way he operates, and I'm used to it. And frankly, it works: I think of Roy and the Dodgers whenever I get sucked into some half-assed argument about race, online or in-person.

Which brings me back to Sunday morning. "Dem bums," I murmured to Roy as I rolled out to hustle a cup of coffee. "Wait'll next year. Reminds me of our chess team."

My mom was already in the kitchen, eating her usual health-nut breakfast: unsweetened yogurt over a pile of unidentifiable grains that looked, and probably tasted, like gravel. She raised an eyebrow but kept silent as I mixed up a tall iced Nescafé with tap water, milk, and a couple of heaping spoons of sugar. (I have Official Parental Permission to drink one cup of coffee per day, but I got it only after a prolonged struggle. Mom and Dad actually forced me to create a PowerPoint presentation to make my case — they're like that. I don't think they were entirely convinced by my facts and graphs, but they appreciated the effort and let it slide. They didn't need to know that most of the Ninth Grade hits Starbuck's every day as soon as the lunch bell rings. Anyhow, if my growth was stunted, so be it: At least they wouldn't need to replace my prized Muji flannels every couple of months.)

Mom could tell right off that I was bummed. She could always read me. Not that it would have been hard: I probably looked like a sad-face emoji.

"Mose, you're upset about something. You want to talk about it?"

Those are Words of Doom for most kids my age. But my mom is actually pretty helpful when we talk things out. She has skills; she's a psychiatric social worker.

I'd already decided not to mention the confrontation outside the bodega. Both parents would go buck nutty; they'd probably drag me around the neighborhood and post the whole story to Facebook so they could find the villain and threaten him with Grievous Bodily Harm. Everyone at school would hear about it and I'd be in for days, maybe weeks, of excruciating embarrassment. I just wanted to put that episode behind me. So I stuck to chess.

"Do you really want to know? We got creamed again by the J. Press mafia. I'm beginning to wonder if it's worth the effort."

I knew what she'd say. "It's worth the effort if you're learning something and spending time with your friends. Besides, you made a big commitment of hours and energy pulling that club together. Your dad and I always like to see you carry through what you've started."

"It may not be up to me," I said. "Seems like the team is falling apart. I'm afraid I'm the only one who really gives a damn anymore."

I told her pretty much the whole sorry story, including Esther throwing mood and P.D. ghosting the final round. (I skipped over the weird vibe I got from Maggie: seemed unimportant at the time.)

Mom heard me out and then got straight to the point as usual. "Break it down, Mose. Why did you start the team in the first place?"

I thought for a moment.

"At the beginning, it was all about me, to be honest. I was trying to be a leader, like the teachers always say we should. But after we started doing tournaments, it was more about the school. I thought Q722 had a chance to do something special, stand out from the crowd. Plus I thought it would be cool for me and my friends to do something together. Like *together* together. Even when we hang out, we're always staring at our phones, like we're in little individual bubbles. I guess I was hoping that the chess team could make a real connection between us."

"From what you tell me, it sounds like you're still trapped in those bubbles."

She took our breakfast things over to the sink to wash up. I did the drying; all the chores in our happy hippie house were distributed communally.

"Maggie's in her own world," she continued. "Esther's preoccupied with the various chips on her shoulder; P.D. is hellbent on proving he's a lone-wolf genius who doesn't need anybody except himself. You're not really a team; you're four individuals running off in four different directions. Does the club meet on a regular basis?"

"Not really," I conceded. "We tried it for a while, but all we were doing was playing skittles in an empty classroom. Might as well just play online."

She took a deep breath. "Mose, you know I don't like to tell you what to do. It's always best when you figure it out for yourself. But I can make a suggestion."

"Go for it."

"Maybe you need to form your own learning community." Uh-oh. Sounded like a concept from Mom's continuing education courses.

"Okay, I'll bite — what's a learning community?"

"It's a collaborative approach to learning — when students get together and organize themselves around a common goal. I'll show you some of the research if you want. Seems to work. You could try meeting on a regular basis; immerse yourselves in chess. Build solidarity. Learn by doing."

"Just what we need," I groaned. "More school."

"To the contrary. I think this might be a way of escaping from the boring classroom drills that you hate so much. It's the opposite of teaching to the test, where you're expected to perform on cue."

Mom hated high-stakes testing, thought it was turning us kids into robots.

"I don't want to sound jargony, but education is really a social process," she continued. "In a learning community, you'd be training each other, inspiring each other, choosing your own goals. It would improve your chess, but the real point is that you'd end up bonding as a team — whether you like it or not."

"But mom, we can't teach each other what we don't know," I objected. "We'd just be running around in circles."

"Agreed. That's why you're going to need to undertake a quest. I think you need to find a coach. Someone with real expertise who isn't a Nazi. Someone who is willing to work with you collaboratively in a way that will inspire you — ideally, somebody with a little charisma. It'll give your friends a reason to show up. In the end, maybe you'll start winning some tournaments."

"So basically, you're telling me I have to find Mister Miyagi."

She laughed. "Pretty much."

"That isn't a quest; that's a labor of Hercules." That was my cue for us to go into our Steve Reeves routine. Mom and I were both heavy Netflix consumers and connoisseurs of so-bad-they're-good B-movies. We both loved the crappy old Italian sword-and-sandals epics, especially the ones starring Reeves, the painfully wooden Schwarzenegger of his day. The dialogue cracked us up, and we had large chunks memorized.

"I can't stand being superior!" I did my best to reproduce the awkward tones of the dubbing booth. "Let me experience the real things, love or hate."

She threw a dish towel over her head and mugged like the Oracle at

Delphi.

"Those are but mortal states, Hercules."

"If it's my immortality that makes me unhappy, then let me do without it."

“Follow your destiny then. But don’t ask for mercy!”

In reply, I popped a lat spread — which isn’t easy when you don’t have any lats. We shared major *jaja.* Then she ruffled my hair, which I hate (though I’d also kind of hate it if she stopped doing it.) “Give it some thought, Hercules. You might find an answer pretty close to home.”

Was that some kind of hint? It sounded like a wisdom nugget from an Afterschool Special, which was unlike my mom. Weird. I shrugged and dropped the subject. Only a few hours left before I started getting stressed out about school tomorrow. Time for some gaming, and maybe a little homework. I could sort all this out later.

3. GRANDMASTER FLEISCH AND THE FURIOUS FIVE

Back in school Monday morning. The first thing I saw was Marco and Steve, a couple of prize dickwits I knew from Middle School, bracing some little kid against a locker. No doubt they were after his lunch money. I stopped and shot them what I hoped was a stone-cold stare.

"*Really*, dudes? Aren't you getting a little old for this Biff Tannen bullshit?"

"You want some too, Middleton?" snarled Marco, the smaller, smarter, and meaner of the two. "Steve here will be happy to oblige."

Damn. Two minutes into the school day and my ass was already on the line. I should have kept my stupid mouth shut, but I guess I was still hurting from Saturday night and looking to compensate for my cowardice. Now I was stuck: I couldn't back down or they'd be harassing me all semester long. The dynamic duo released their victim and squared off on me. Another crisis loomed.

All of a sudden, Marco and Steve froze, looking past me over my shoulder, slack-jawed and goggle-eyed. I heard a sharp fingersnap and the unmistakably sinister voice of P.D.: "Step off, muppets." My assailants backpedaled slowly, flexing and posturing, telegraphing tough-guy body language in a failed attempt to save face. When they were at a safe distance, they booked it. Predictably, Marco yelled "Later, faggots!" before disappearing around a corner. (P.D. was gay and didn't care who knew it.)

P.D. emitted an evil laugh and turned to me. "Those dime store villains are not the most convincing argument for heterosexuality, my lad. Anyway, what's behind today's fiasco? You're playing Moses the Lawgiver? Coming down from the mount to smite the unrighteous?"

"This young man" — I nodded toward the kid — "was getting the shakedown from 722's Brain Trust. I intervened in my usual heroic fashion."

"What's your name, kid?" P.D. asked quietly. P.D. intimidated all the Mean Boys and would-be gangstas, but he was invariably kind to the weak.

"I'm Zamir. Zamir Hoxha." (It sounded like "Hoja"; only later did he tell me how to spell it.) "I'm new here." No kidding. He was small for a freshman, with dark curly hair and milk-white skin. Neatly dressed — too neatly — in what we used to call "school clothes" back in K-6. Cords, collared shirt, leather kicks. Primed for victimhood.

"You can call me P.D. And this is Moses, who desperately wants to be my sidekick. Anybody gives you any trouble, just summon Mose. Then he'll come running, screaming, to me."

P.D. tipped a finger to the brim of his ballcap and sauntered down the hall, leaving me with Zamir, who was shouldering a backpack that looked heavier than he was.

"Let me guess," I said. "You're Albanian, aren't you?

He flashed a shy smile. "How did you know?" He still had his accent. Most of the kids in my neighborhood start out with some kind of accent, but by high school everybody sounds pretty much the same, able to spew fake-ass hip-hop argot at a moment's notice. So he was bound to stand out, and probably not in a good way. Somewhere in the halls of 722, I imagined, some other geeky kid was having the best day of his life: No longer the biggest nerd in school, he'd have someone else to sneer at from now on.

"The name tipped me off," I answered. "Not so strange. Seems like all the doormen in JH are from there, so I can usually recognize an Albanian name."

"You are the chess guy, right?"

"Well, yeah." I was kind of flattered. Maybe I was acquiring some credibility after all, even if it was only among my fellow dweebs. "You play?"

"Yes, and I would very much like to join your club." Uh-oh. After last weekend's debacle, I wasn't really sure whether the club still existed. So I put him off.

"The club is kind of on hold right now, but I'll get back to you, okay?" I hitched up my backpack and headed for my first class with a perfunctory wave. "We'll play a game some time."

But I wasn't going to lose Zamir so easily. A couple of hours later I saw him again in my Italian class, where it was immediately clear that he was much more advanced than the rest of us. I'd forgotten that Albania was just a stone's throw from Italy, and I didn't then realize that most Albanians could speak at least a little Italian, and maybe a little Greek and Russian too. (As far as knowledge of Albania went, I was probably way ahead of most Americans in just being able to locate the country on a map.) The teacher was schooling us immersion-style, and I was struggling to follow. I was in a mid-morning trough, craving a shot of caffeine and a lungful of vaporous satisfaction: *Non capisco un cazzo.*

Why Italian, you ask? Most of the kids took Chinese, because they assumed it would be a slick career move, or Spanish, because they thought (wrongly) that it would be easy. Me, I had no better reason for choosing Italian than my love for cheesy movies. After exhausting the Hercules flicks, I branched out into Italian horror — mad shit that broke all the rules — and obscure Spaghetti Westerns. Most of this stuff was dubbed, badly, into English, but just following the relateds on YouTube took me into new realms. Turned out my favorite Western villain, Gian Maria Volonté, was not only the All-Time Master of the Death Stare but was also considered the greatest Italian actor of his day. Mom nudged me, subtly, in directions she approved of. Before I knew it, I was watching Volonté in subtitled arthouse films and tripping on the musical sound of the dialogue. So I figured I could fulfill my language requirement and feed my obsessions at the same time. But the going was tough: This wasn't just passively consuming movies; I had to speak and study, and frankly it made my brain hurt.

Bell rang; I was beelining for Starbuck's but Zamir intercepted me.

"Moses! Hey, Moses!" I winced as heads swiveled. He was shrill to say the least.

"Call me Mose. *Please.*"

"Mose, when do you want to play? I'm ready any time."

I remembered I'd promised him a game. Damn. He was so eager I just couldn't stand to let him down. "We'll play online tonight. What's your handle?"

Looking downcast, he informed me that his family had only just moved in, and he wasn't wired up yet. So online was out, at least till his family got wifi, and of course neither of us had brought a set to school. But the weather was weirdly warm for late January, and I had an inspiration.

"Meet me outside after the last bell and we'll go down to Travers Park. Someone will probably give us a game, and then we can play winners." Whereupon I Usain Bolted for the coffee shop, desperate for my fix. "*Ciao!*"

I ground through the rest of the school day, guzzling from the firehose of knowledge and trying not to watch the clock too closely. After the final period, Zamir was waiting on the steps outside, actually bouncing up and down with enthusiasm. I felt like I'd just picked up a new puppy from the pound. Part of me — the part of me that I despise — was signaling that I should steer clear; hanging out with the dimpiest kid in 722 was not going to do much for my already lackluster rep. But then I remembered P.D., my idol, whose unassailable cool was grounded in the fact that he couldn't give a flying dookey what anybody thought of him. *Possono baciarmi il culo.*

"Let's do it." We advanced parkward.

Travers looked pretty bleak when we got there. No one on the swings; a couple of kids playing a half-hearted game of horse under the hoops. At first

I thought the chess tables were unoccupied, but as we got closer I could see one lone oldun off in the corner, squinting at a complex position with a cig dangling from his lips.

We approached and I realized it was Viktor, the reputed grandmaster whom I'd never dared to challenge. Well, here was my chance. I swallowed hard.

"Hey, man — looking for a game?"

Close up, I could see that he wasn't the clapped-out homeless dude I'd always taken him for. He was about a million years old but decked: schnazz wool overcoat, perfectly round tortoiseshell eyeglasses, engraved cigarette case that had to be silver. He looked up from the board, slowly, and surveyed us both with a penetrating gaze. I won't lie: He freaked me out for a minute. He had some kind of witchy presence; I felt like he was taking inventory of my pathetic little soul. He frowned.

"When addressing your elders, is not customary to introduce yourself first?" He had a heavy Russian accent but spoke English better than I did, except for dropping the occasional article. Me, I was (*vocab alert!*) chagrined.

"Sorry, um, sir. I'm Moses Middleton and this is my friend Zamir Hoxha. We don't have a set and we're hoping to play some chess."

"That … is a possibility." He offered his hand in a sweeping gesture and announced, in a suddenly thunderous voice: "I am Viktor Fleischmann. I am the history of chess." Theatrical pause. "You are perhaps the future."

His delivery was hella dramatic, like a Bond villain. Later I would realize that this was just his style. Early on, he'd cultivated a larger-than-life attitude as a way of intimidating opponents. Eventually he just *became* the role he liked to play, like when Moms tells you to stop crossing your eyes or they'll get stuck that way. At the time, though, the Goldfinger bit was mad menacing. I caught Zamir's eye; he looked even more terrified than I was.

"Queen odds?" Viktor offered, setting up the pieces so deftly that I was reminded of the three-card monte wizards on Broadway. I gulped and took a seat while Zamir looked on.

"Since you have a small advantage, Mr. Middleton, you will do me the courtesy of allowing me to play white."

I was okay with that. I was still petro but I figured I could beat just about anybody with queen odds. It was just a matter of trading down till the nine-point handicap became unbeatable.

We opened with e4-e5; so far so good. Then he pushed his king's bishop pawn. King's Gambit. I knew the opening pretty well but got spooked; figured he must be laying a trap. I declined, but spaced out and played d6, the wrong response. No problem, I reassured myself, my advantage is still massive. As we pushed and traded pawns for a spell, wrestling for control of the center, he made his moves almost instantaneously, like speed chess. I began to feel like he was anticipating everything I was going to do; he might as well have been moving my pieces *for* me. Just seven moves in, he had both his knights in play and my king's pawn was isolated. He threw a g5 at me, attacking my queen, and suddenly he was chasing her around the board. It happened incredibly fast and my head was spinning: Rook, bishops, and knight converged on my king while my queen — my supposedly insurmountable advantage — had to sit it out, powerless to intervene. Checkmate in 12 moves. Like a bad dream.

And there I was again, elbows on table, head cradled in hands, surveying a losing position. "That was pretty humiliating," I said. "Throw me a bone here, Mr. Fleishmann. Are you really an international grandmaster?"

"I was — before I went mad. Didn't your mother tell you about me?"

This was getting weird. How did he know my mom? I stammered a no.

"Dr. Rose Middleton is your mother, correct?" I confirmed this, though she wasn't a medical doctor, just a PhD.

"I was sent to her after I was locked up in a mental institution. She was guardian angel; cured me of madness."

"She got you on meds?" I asked.

"No, Mr. Middleton; she got me *off* meds! I am still perhaps an unusual character" — here he smiled thinly — "but my brain is now functioning. You may ask her about my past if you wish." He shuffled the pieces back into position, once again leaving his queen aside. "Now, it is Mr. Hoxha's turn. Queen odds again"?

The moment Zamir sat down and positioned himself over the board his anxiety disappeared. In fact, he looked positively blissful. I knew right away that he'd popped into The Zone, the place that was so elusive for me. Viktor ran the King's Gambit again, but Zamir accepted. He calmly developed his pieces and fended off the sweeping attacks with which I had been so swiftly crushed. Viktor chipped away at Zamir's advantage, creating fantastically complicated positions that worked in his favor. By the time the endgame was reached, white was up a pawn and black offered his resignation. Zamir had taken the L, but this was a super-respectable loss against a grandmaster, even with queen odds. TBH, I was a little bit jealous. At the same time, I was getting excited: Could this kid take the team to the next level?

Despite his loss, Zamir wasn't devastated like me; he was actually beaming. "Thank you for the game, Mr. Viktor!"

Viktor raised an eyebrow shot me a look. "Mr. Middleton — perhaps I may call you Moses? — you should learn from this boy, and not just in chess. He is a true gentleman."

Chagrined again. Of course, Viktor didn't comprehend that gentlemanly behavior wasn't going to get anybody very far in an urban high school. Zamir needed to toughen up, I figured, but when I thought of him losing that sunny, eager innocence, it gave me a little twist in the pit of my stomach.

"So, Mr. Fleischmann," I said, trying to sound as gentlemanly as I could.

"Are we any good?"

He thought for a moment.

"Mr. Hoxha — Zamir — is possibly *very* good, but I would need to observe him further. You, Moses, may have potential also. But you let your mind wander; you do not concentrate."

He could see I was crestfallen, and he continued, in a milder tone: "Do not despair. This is a problem even for best players. Like me." He gestured toward his cigarette case.

"You see the picture engraved here? That is Alexander Pushkin, greatest Russian poet." He took a deep breath, cast his eyes skyward, and reeled off a musical chunk of verse.

"What was that?" Zamir asked. "It is about chess, I know, but I could only understand a little."

"It is a minor episode from very long and very famous poem. A boy is committing an appalling blunder because he is getting dreamy about his girlfriend. My teammates gave me this little object to commemorate a stupid blunder I once committed that cost our team a tournament." (I could relate.) "It was meant to remind me that I must always concentrate."

I made a mental note to look up this poem when I got home; there's no telling what kind of trivia will help me when I start taking the Big Tests. *I'll take Russian Poets for $500, Alex.*

I checked the time on my phone; I was due at home to set the table and throw together a Big Salad.

"Excuse me, Mr. Fleischmann, but I gotta go. We'll be seeing you soon, okay?"

He waved his hand dismissively, but he was smiling. "Good evening, boys. You may return in future for more punishment if you so desire."

We said our goodbyes and left the park. Zamir was still getting to know the neighborhood, so I walked him home. Turned out he lived in a borderline-swank high-rise just outside JH, where his dad was — yep — a doorman.

As we stood outside, Zamir asked me for a couple of English pointers. "Should I be calling him Mr. Viktor or Mr. Fleischmann?"

"In the US we'd say 'Mr. Fleischmann' if we were being formal." I had a brainwave. "But privately I'm going to think of him as Grandmaster Fleisch."

Zamir wasn't picking up on the reference, so I explained.

"You know, like Grandmaster Flash. It's old-school hip-hop. The *oldest* school." I knew the rap classics from browsing my dad's bizarre CD collection, which was about equally split between Brooklyn turntablism and grand opera. "Hey, if I can get the chess team started again, you can join and there'll be five players." I was thriving on the riff. "See, a couple of us are furious all the time, and the rest of us have good reason to be."

"They'll call us" — pregnant pause; WWE announcer voice —

"*Grandmaster Fleisch and the Furious Five*!"

Crickets. Zamir looked puzzled; he was a long way from getting a handle on the pop culture obsessions that my classmates and I shared. A few months of immersion in high school would fix that problem, no doubt. Soon he'd be quoting bad movies and Photoshopping his own memes. Meanwhile, my lame joke landed like the Hindenburg.

Zamir and I parted ways and I headed home, thinking hard about the day's events. Clearly, Mom had been pulling strings behind the scenes. She'd set me up to go in search of our Mister Miyagi, then vectored me in the right direction. Was I being manipulated? Sure. Did I care? Kind of, but if she'd handed me a solution to my problem it would be hard to stay mad. I figured I'd give it shot.

4. COMMIE PLOTS

When I got home, everything was in a state of bustle and disorder. Van parked outside, boxes stacked in the hall, Dad in a paint-stained T-shirt directing traffic on the stairs. Obviously we had a new tenant. I checked with Dad; turned out one of Dante's coworkers had lost her apartment and needed a place to stay for a while. Didn't bother me; this kind of thing happened at our place all the time. The only possible drawback was the bathroom situation. Despite all our revolving tenants, we were never really short of space as such. But bathrooms required extra attention to privacy and gender issues. The two married couples — my parents; Mallika and Ritwik — had the en suite bathrooms. At the moment I was sharing one that opened off the second-floor hallway with Julian and Dante. That left the small first-floor bathroom for our latest addition. Fortunately, Dad had installed a shower in there a couple of months ago, so everything appeared copacetic.

I met the newbie an hour later during another communal chowdown around the reconditioned industrial workbench that served as our dinner table. (Tonight we'd had my hands-down favorite, Dante's super-spicy chicken stew with heaps of rice and beans; I ate so much that I had to undo the top button of my Carhartts.) Her name was Allegra. Couldn't help noticing that she was, ahem, attractive — hey, I'm 14 years old and I'd be lying if I pretended I wasn't hyper-aware of hotness — but she looked to be in her early 20s and in any case was way out of my league. I didn't learn much about her; her English was a little shaky and she was probably overwhelmed by the noisy enthusiasm of our freewheeling supper club.

Afterwards, Mom and I were together on bussing detail, so I had my chance to confront her about Viktor. Partly pissed-off and partly grateful, I tried to keep things light with the Steve Reeves bit.

"By the Gods, woman! You have deceived me!" I brandished a wooden spoon like Hercules' club.

"Alas, you have uncovered my sinister scheme, Hercules. Seriously though, I thought you two were a natural pair. Shared interests."

I pumped her for Viktor's backstory, first assuring her that he'd given me permission to ask. (She never talked about her clients without their okay: confidentiality and professional ethics and all that.)

"I'm pretty sure he was an important Russian chess player," she began. "You could look him up."

I already had. He was a strong but not dazzling player, a contemporary of the great Anatoly Karpov. He played on the bomb-ass teams of the 60s and 70s, back when the Soviet Chess Championship was the most important tournament in the world. His peak Elo was around 2600 at a time when Bobby Fischer's 2785 was considered untouchable. (This was before all that fool ratings inflation rolled in, when suddenly a bunch of guys you never heard of were ranked higher than Karpov or Korchnoi.) For some reason, though, Viktor faded from the chess scene in the late 80s. I couldn't find a record of any rated games after 1991. I mentioned this to my mom.

"Stands to reason," she said. "He claims he lost his marbles on the day they lowered the red flag over the Kremlin for the last time. Everything he believed in, everything he'd struggled for, was swept away almost overnight. He felt his life had lost all meaning. He was competing at a tournament in Paris when he got the news and he just lost it; wandered away from the hotel and disappeared. He became homeless in the broadest sense of the word."

"Wow, so he was a legit Communist?"

She shrugged. "Maybe you can ask him when you get to know him a little better. But you know that's not a dirty word in our household. My grandparents were lifelong Party members, and my mom and dad are definitely Reds, though not of the card-carrying variety."

(I loved this. Grandpa and Grandma were subversives! Suddenly I could see them with new eyes: When they weren't birdwatching or power-walking the mall, maybe they were secretly plotting the overthrow of the capitalist order. Wicked.)

Mom poured herself a glass of white and I followed her into the living room, where we settled on the sofa in front of the TV monitor. Dad was already there, sprawled in the thrift-shop armchair and watching an opera video. Sounded like *Aida*, which I knew had something to do with slavery — not really my kind of beats, but I was picking up on the opera scene through osmosis. Julian, meanwhile, was sitting cross-legged on the old Persian carpet, balancing a sketchbook on his knees while he listened. Typical artsy-fartsy scene *chez* Middleton. I multi-tasked, half-following the opera while we talked. Good for my Italian, I figured.

"Apparently Viktor lived on the streets for years, floating around Europe," Mom continued. "Then some relatives in New York managed to track him down and arranged to bring him here. He's living in an extra bedroom in his nephew's apartment in Woodside."

When Viktor came to town he was still pretty messed up, she told me, making scenes in public and creating problems with the landlord. So Mom, who worked for an agency that provided community mental health services, got involved. She helped wean him off some heavy-duty psychiatric drugs that were fuzzing out his brain so he couldn't play chess. Apart from that, she just talked to him with respect and empathy; made some practical suggestions. She was good at that.

"He's improved, a lot, but he's still lonely. Doesn't have a purpose in life."

"Right: and that's where *I* come in," I said, still a little testy. "You can be really manipulative, you know?"

"Sorry — but frankly, not sorry. I thought it could be a win-win if I could get you guys together. And nobody's forcing either of you." She smiled and threw her arm around my shoulder. "Foolish mortal, what good is your irresistible strength unless you use it in service of justice?"

I melted; I couldn't ever stay mad at her, though I tried really hard sometimes. We considered my next moves. I needed to talk to Viktor, see if he'd be willing to set up a session with the club. Then I had to canvass the other team members and try to persuade them to make the meeting.

"But we'll need to pay Viktor, right?" I could already see that money was going to be an issue — it always was — but Mom didn't seem fazed.

"See if he'll give you guys a free lesson to start; we can discuss how to compensate him for his time if it works out."

"And how do I make sure everyone shows up?"

"Just say the magic word."

I cackled, knowing what was coming. "You mean — ?"

"Yep, pizza. Your dad and I will spring for it."

This sounded like a plan. We fell silent and Dad, still engrossed in his opera, spoke up. "Settle down for a minute, kiddies, and watch this. It's the best part."

Aida, the slave heroine, was singing a tune so sweet and sad that even I was swept up for a minute. I followed the subtitles:

Oh blue skies, oh sweet native breezes,
where the morning of my life shone peacefully.

She was singing about Africa I guess, but I found myself thinking about Viktor. Viktor and the USSR.

O my country, never more will I see you!
Never more, never more will I see you!

That sorrowful music was still on autoplay in my head as I went upstairs to log an hour of homework, then an hour (okay, maybe two) of online speed chess. Before shutting down the laptop, I did a quick search on Pushkin. I had to browse around for a while, but I was pretty sure the poem Viktor quoted was *Eugene Onegin* — which, coincidentally, was the source material for my dad's favorite opera.

In the poem a guy experiences total vapor lock while playing shawtie; he captures his own rook. When I checked Pushkin out, I discovered something else that blew me away: His great grandfather was a Black African slave who somehow rose to the rank of major-general at the court of Peter the Great, probably due to his military engineering genius. Slavery, chess, opera, race: It felt weird, like different pieces of a mysterious and complicated puzzle were falling into place.

Later, falling asleep, I had some Deep Thoughts. About how every part of my life seemed to be connected to every other part, and to the lives of other people, living and dead, people who were always lurking in the background, invisibly shaping the world and my place in it. Reminded me of something my dad had once said about interconnectedness: Every time you take a breath, it's a mathematical certainty that you're inhaling molecules that were also inhaled by Julius Caesar or Jesus Christ.

I realized I was about to get rabbit-holed by the vastness and complexity of the universe, like when you stare at the stars too long, so I tried to chill by running through some chess positions in my head. Chess was reassuring, somehow: You always start with the same 64 squares, the same pieces and pawns, the same clear set of rules that everyone agrees on and understands the same way. At the outset, it's perfectly ordered and beautiful, a moment of pure potential frozen in time. It's only after you make a move that things turn to shit.

5. ZUGZWANG

The next morning was Tuesday. The chess club had a regular room reserved on Thursday after hours. Not much time. I would need to make a series of fast, aggressive moves to get the club back on track.

I recruited Zamir right before our Italian class. As I expected, it was no problem whatsoever; he'd be there with tubular bells on, kitted up and ready for action.

Maggie next. I caught up with her after the Algebra II class we shared. With her mop of jet-black hair hanging loose around pale, delicate features, she looked exceptionally fine that day; my adolescent heart skipped a couple of beats when she favored me with a smile. Breathlessly I rattled off the backstory and the pitch. Was she up for Thursday night?

To my surprise, her face fell. "I would love to, but I'm not sure I can make it."

Strange. Maggie never said no to chess. "C'mon, Maggie, please. It's an unbelievable opportunity. We're going to be trained by a real live grandmaster." I went for the personal approach. "I *need* you there."

She cast her eyes downward, blinking, and replied in a voice so soft and rapid that I could barely follow her. "Mose-I-am-so-sorry-but-I-have-to-go." Then she bolted off down the hall.

I was gobsmacked. Stood frozen for a moment, mouth hanging open. I only began to recover when a leering Marco zoomed past, throwing me the finger and mouthing: "Be seeing you, fag." I rolled my eyes. There was too much going on in my life right then to worry about empty threats — *hopefully* empty — from that pitiful excuse for a hard guy. I filed away the Maggie issue for later consideration and planned my next move.

I'd already promised two people that they were going to get training from a GM, so the next step was pretty crucial: I had to get Viktor firmly on board. At lunchtime I hustled over to Travers and there he was, once again hunched over the corner table, huffing nicotine through one of those savage Russian cigarettes, the kind with a cardboard tube attached instead of a filter.

"Ah, it is young Mr. Lensky." I realized he was referring to the guy who blunders in the Pushkin poem.

"Good morning, Mr. Fleischmann. If you don't mind, I think I'm going to try *not* to be Lensky — because he ends up getting capped by his best friend."

For the first time since I'd met him, he cracked a full-on smile, exposing a set of uneven teeth that were not exactly white, more like earth tones. I was jazzed: I'd actually managed to make a good impression, which doesn't happen very often.

"You have hidden depths, Moses. Perhaps I can interest you in a game?"

I explained that I was due in school in a few minutes and quickly sketched out the proposal that Mom and I had cooked up.

"I guess maybe it's presumptuous for a high school team to ask for help from a grandmaster, but I was hoping you'd do us the honor."

He looked skyward for a minute as he exhaled a long column of acrid smoke.

"I will do this, if only because of a debt I owe your mother. But it must be a serious lesson. I will expect full attention from everyone. And I would like each of you to bring score sheets from your last few games. I will analyze and see how strong you are."

I gave him the where and when, then broached the issue of money. As Mom had suggested, I asked whether he could give us a free session to start. He nodded, chuckled.

"It is just like your American drugs: First time is always free."

We exchanged cell numbers and I raced schoolward, copping a hasty vape and a bag of steamed momos from the Tibetan stand on 37th Avenue.

Next stop was the vice principals' office. I needed her official sign-off to get Viktor into the building for club meetings; otherwise, the administration — basically a useless gaggle of paranoids and petty authoritarians — would probably decide he was a pedo and call the cops. I dreaded this woman. Stacey Sanprudencio, an administrative gunslinger who liked to call herself the Chief Operating Officer, had swooped down on 722 after we crapped the bed on our annual DOE report card. You know the type: professional updo; no facial expressions; able to spew reams of CorpSpeak at a moment's notice. She'd scammed some kind of online EdD and insisted on being addressed as *Doctor* Sanprudencio. Among ourselves we called her Doctor Evil.

As she never tired of reminding us, she was charged with cleaning up our act and improving our "metrics." So far I'd managed to avoid any direct interactions with her, but I knew her reputation. She was phony woke, a gaslighting specialist who trapped kids with arbitrary rules while simulating concern.

She was wary at first — she just presumed that any kid who approached her with an idea was running a grift — but I'd come prepared. I handed her a printout of a *New York Times* article about Chess in the Schools, one that focused on the tournament prowess of a Bed-Stuy charter. A glowing spotlight was thrown on a crusading vice principal who had adopted chess as his pet project. He'd brought in a disciplinarian coach and built a strong team in one of the city's poorest districts. The write-up was expertly calibrated to appeal to *Times* readers; chess, it was implied, had a civilizing influence on unruly natives. I figured the good doctor would be unable to resist an opportunity to bask in this kind of publicity.

I was right. After reading the story she suddenly became my biggest fan; she made a point of pretending that she'd championed our chess club from Day One, which was utter bullshit. (In fact I'd had to do everything myself, encountering resistance and suspicion from the administration every step of the way.) But I played along. Fine with me if she needed to take credit; just give us our club, our room, and our coach.

There was, of course, a catch.

"There's something I need you to understand, Moses. We're a multi-output organization that is laser-focused on enhancing our core competencies. Extracurricular activity is a privilege that thrives on individual accountability."

I smiled and nodded, trying to project enthusiastic obedience as she hosed me down with jargon.

"Horacio Morales is a member of your club I believe." She meant P.D. "He has a marked tendency to display uncooperative and defiant behaviors. In particular his attendance record is a matter of concern — *compassionate* concern — to this institution. He needs to let us nurture him, if necessary with tough love. Therefore his participation in your club is conditional on his prosocial behavior. Do I make myself clear?"

She did. P.D. had to make a show of bending the knee or he'd be out on his ass. As I left her office she arranged her features into a lizard-like grimace; I believe she was simulating a smile.

"Make us proud, Moses." She actually pumped her fist. Awkwardly.

By this point I was so comprehensively doused in horseshit that I felt like taking a shower. Instead I marched through my remaining classes. Throughout the afternoon, P.D. was nowhere to be found. No huge surprise. As Doctor Evil well knew, he was a habitual truant; his style in any course was to skip most of the sessions, then parachute in for the final exam and ace it. I'd shoot him a text after school and hope for a response; otherwise I'd have to wait till tomorrow. Maybe he'd deign to drop in for a class or two.

Esther was a different kind of challenge. We didn't share any classes and I didn't run into her all day. Technically we weren't allowed to text during school hours, but I messaged her on the sly during a trip to the john. No answer. So when the final bell rang I swallowed hard, steeled myself, and jogged over to Esther's place.

She lived in a neatly kept brick rowhouse, where her mom, a nurse, tended a vegetable garden in the postage-stamp yard out front. The place was more or less identical to the $2 million joints over in the Historic District, but it was maybe one-quarter the price just because it sat on the wrong side of 37th Avenue, across the border from Wypipo Land. That should tell you something about New York real estate.

I could hear her playing exercises on her violin as I mounted the stoop and rang the bell. That was Esther's life: practicing, fencing, homework, chores, streaming a corny romance flick every now and then just to keep from losing her mind. She had to be the hardest-working kid in 722.

She opened the door with fiddle and bow in hand, looking distracted and a little irritated.

"Mose, what the *hell* are you doing here? I don't remember inviting you."

I apologized for the interruption and told her we needed to talk for a couple of minutes; she rolled her eyes, sighed and let me in. She seated me in her kitchen, offered me a slice of Haitian butter cake and started coffee in one of those little Italian moka pots. This was how she was raised: She was constitutionally incapable of letting a guest into the house, welcome or not, without breaking out the noms.

"Okay, Mose, this had better be good. Getting in my face when I'm practicing is a major blunder. We're talking double question-mark."

I should explain about Esther and her violin. A few years ago, she casually picked up one of her mom's French-language books — it's a trilingual household, French, Creole, and English — and instantly tripped out on the cover picture: a painting of a handsome brother with a sword, all G'd up, 18th Century style, in a powdered wig and a ruffled neckcloth. It was the biography of guy from Guadeloupe named Joseph Bologne, the Chevalier de Saint-Georges, who became a superstar of revolutionary France: expert swordsman, military hero, concert violinist and classical composer. He was Black in the Roy Campanella sense, with a white father and a Black mother. (They called him the "Black Mozart," but Esther won't hear of it: she says Wolfgang M. should be called the "White Bologne.") Unlike the Campanellas, though, his parents were nobody's idea of a love story. His mom was his dad's slave, so you'd have to say she was raped; no way she could have said no to a man who literally owned her. Still, his dad loved him enough to acknowledge him as his son and sent him off to France, where he mastered everything he learned and became the Coolest Guy Ever. I'd never heard of the man till Esther filled me in; made me wonder how many other sensationally accomplished PoC have been flushed down the memory hole.

Anyhow, Esther read the book and fell in love with the man; she pretty much wanted to *be* him. And once Esther made up her mind, she was an irresistible force. Her mom agreed to smash the piggy bank, quite literally, and scrambled to pay for violin lessons and fencing camp. Fortunately, Esther was so good with both sword and fiddle that she made it into the scholarship pipeline before her mom went broke. Now she fences with a private-school team and makes music with the NYC Youth Orchestra. She plays a fufu Cremona fiddle on loan from some billionaire's collection. She wants to get into Juilliard and you'd be a fool to bet against her.

Between huge bites of the cake — it was the kind flavored with rum; trust me, it's the Michael Jordan GOAT of desserts — I briefed her on my Viktor project; told her it wouldn't feel right if she wasn't there; mentioned the pizza.

"I challenge you to attend." I produced what I thought was my ace in the hole. "Surely the Chevalier de Saint-Georges would never have declined a gentlemanly challenge."

"Mose, that's the cheapest kind of manipulation. As I informed you last weekend, I haven't a moment to waste on your puerile chess adventures." She was, of course, rocking the BBC accent. She laid her fiddle in its case, rubbed the rosin dust off her hands with a paper towel, and spoke normally. "But I am going to say yes, just this once, because otherwise you're going to make sad-puppy eyes at me and I'll probably throw up."

That was unexpected, to say the least. Did Esther actually give more than one rat's ass about my feelings? Were there limits to her contempt? Seemed impossible to believe, but I figured I'd think about it later; now it was time for my next move.

"What about Maggie? When I asked her, she kind of weirded out and wouldn't commit. She practically ran away from me down the hall. You know her a lot better than I do: What is going on in her head?"

Suddenly Esther looked grim. Even grimmer than usual, that is.

"I'm not supposed to tell you any of this, and I probably shouldn't, so I need you to swear you didn't hear this from me."

"I swear by the beard of Zeus!"

"No joke, Mose, and GTFO with your Hercules bullshit. This is absolutely confidential; the conversation we're about to have did not happen, understand?"

I nodded, contrite, and did my best to project sincerity. When Esther was serious, she was *serious*.

"She says her uncle is pressuring her to drop all her extra-curricular stuff. I think he wants her isolated. So he can control her. See, Maggie's dad died a couple of years ago, and she and her mom have been scraping by ever since. Her uncle lives with them. Evidently he's a complete dick. He was supposed to help pay the rent, but he just sits around the apartment all day, drinking forties and watching tv. Lately he's been perving on her — coming up behind her and massaging her shoulders, grilling her about her sex life. Last week he asked whether she wanted to watch some porn with him. Every girl knows this pattern: It's only a matter of time before he tries something."

"What about her mom?"

"She loves Maggie but lately she's never home. She was some kind of scientific researcher in China, but she and her husband wanted to open a business here. They were chasing the American Dream I guess. But when he died, all those plans collapsed. She has debt that she can't service. Worse, she overstayed her visa so technically she's undocumented. Evidently she's had to do some shady shit just to put food on the table. I have the feeling she might be working at an AMP."

If you don't know what that means, it stands for Asian Massage Parlor. You can see them all over Roosevelt Avenue and Flushing; the women are forced to stand outside and solicit customers. The way they're treated is disgusting. My mom has counseled a couple of victims, so she knows the story. Women get trafficked from China, then the pimps take their passports and force them to work off their debts. It's illegal but the cops never do anything about it; they're probably on the take. All this happens right out in the open, yet somehow the gentrifying hordes manage to stay serenely blind to it while they're scoring diversity points by sampling the area's delightful ethnic cuisine.

"WTF?" I was torqued. "So nights and weekends Maggie's trapped in a little apartment with Chester the Molester? That's bullshit. We have to report it."

"That's exactly what I told Maggie, but she said absolutely not. Once the authorities get involved, you know they're bound to find out about her mom. They'll take Maggie away, make her a ward of the court, put her into The System." She looked me straight in the eye and banged the table to get her words across: "We. Cannot. Let. That. Happen."

I got her point. We all knew kids who were in foster care. They hated it. Some got a lucky placement with a relatively sane and kindhearted family. Most ended up in foster care mills with guardians who were milking the system for money. Some were basically household slaves, doing all the chores in exchange for a life without pocket money or decent clothes. Some of them would start boosting just to get a presentable pair of sneakers to wear to school. Some got molested. None of them felt like they had rights or choices; shitheel foster dads and indifferent judges made all their life decisions for them. For many, Child Protective Services was just an on-ramp into Juvie Justice, and ultimately the slam or the streets. Once you're in The System, it's almost impossible to get out.

"Spitballing here, but does he have his papers? Couldn't we call Immigration on him?"

"Same problem. Immigration would go after Maggie's mom, too. Besides, I don't hold with snitching on people, especially to ICE. Way too much of that shit goes on in this neighborhood already."

"So what are we going to do about it?"

"I dunno, Mose. I'm stymied. I feel like my hands are tied. Apply your matchless intellect to the problem; maybe you can figure something out."

It crossed my mind that we were in zugzwang, that maddening situation in chess where you can't just stand pat but any move you make is going to be disastrous. And somehow it was on me to find a brilliancy that could break open the position.

She picked up her bow, a clear signal that it was time for me to move on. So I had to make an abrupt transition.

"Um, can you make it Thursday?" Tried not to sound too whiny. "And can you try to bring Maggie along? It might make her feel better."

"I'll see what I can do. Maybe I can come up with a cover story that will fly with Funny Uncle. But no promises."

Leaving Esther to her scales, I hit the street and checked my phone. Had a message from P.D.:

>Roger that, ragazzo. Will come, if only 4 za.

So that was him sorted, or so I hoped.

Later I found Zamir online. He still didn't have wifi but he'd downloaded an app and was now grinding phone chess like the wild Albanian berserker that hid beneath his mild exterior. We logged a few games of rapid. The kid was *good.* He took me for three out of four, with one draw, and messed up my hard-earned Elo. I looked at his stats and could see he'd be surpassing me within days. So much for the satisfactions of mentorship.

Crazy day. I'd brute-forced my way through a connected series of problems; would have been congratulating myself if I hadn't encountered a much more grievous problem, one that could not be hacked or finessed. Something had to be done about Maggie, and I was far from sure that I was the right guy to do it.

6. PIZZA PARTY

Thursday afternoon clocked in and I sprang into action. A few minutes before five, I grabbed a bunch of boards and enlisted a battalion of Staunton Warriors; laid them out in the now-empty lunch room I'd reserved for the club. Ordered pizzas in a variety of styles — mega-meat for me and P.D; a couple of plains; a veggie special in case there were garden gobblers among us — and waited, a little nervously, for the gang to show up.

Zamir was first to arrive, of course. He was wearing an exquisitely cheugy T-shirt that said, in huge block letters: "I AM BECOMING WINNER." (Nope, no "A.") He must have brought it with him from Albania. It killed me; I immediately wanted one just like it. Ironically. OK, maybe not so ironically.

He didn't have any scoresheets to show; he'd only just joined USCF and hadn't played any over-the-board tournaments. So we logged into his online chess account and I printed out a few recent games, carefully omitting the ones where he'd stripwaxed some loser whose handle was Mose722.

To my relief, Esther glided through the door with Maggie in tow. I managed a quick, quiet exchange with Esther: Turned out Maggie had told her creepy uncle that she had a compulsory review session for an upcoming state test. He grilled her for a couple of minutes but in the end, he'd bought it.

Maggie looked cheerier. I asked her how she was doing and she flashed a big smile — I won't lie; that smile always blitzed my insides like a hit of something illegal. We did small talk for a couple of beats; then I introduced Zamir to her and Esther. Maggie was, of course, sweet to him, and Esther did her best approximation of being nice, which was basically a matter of refraining from stone-cold rudeness. I'd already clued him that getting on Esther's good side took some doing but was well worth the effort.

Then Viktor arrived, still attired in his flash overcoat and smelling like a field of fragrant tobacco. He swept through the door dramatically and executed a Russian military salute, elbow back, palm down, fingers at the temple. Introductions ensued. Viktor collected our score sheets and whipped through them hella brisk. Like a speed reader he was absorbing the games at a glance, occasionally raising an eyebrow or muttering a Russian word under his breath. He came to the end of the stack, looked up, and addressed himself to the group.

"There is potential here, my young friends, but far too many blunders and much dubious strategy. I am nevertheless confident that each of you can improve if that is what you desire."

He pulled Maggie's scoresheets from the pile.

"Miss Wang — may I call you Maggie?"

She nodded.

"You know your openings and you have an impressive ability to construct a positional defense. For this reason, as I'm sure you already know, you are strongest with black pieces. However, you lack aggression. You find it difficult to capitalize on your opponent's mistakes. A good tactician can mount a dangerous attack against you while you are still developing your pieces."

Maggie looked stricken. Her lower lip trembled; for a minute I worried that she was going to lose it. But Viktor's expression softened in consolation.

"All this can be fixed, my dear. You have the makings of an able player."

Maggie instantly looked radiant and I nearly sighed with relief. So far, so good. Next victim.

"Miss Toussaint — may I call you Esther?" Esther nodded; Viktor was a real stickler for etiquette. "I surmise that your rating is lower than it should be, given the tactical skill you often display. What is holding you back is, for want of a better word, sloppiness. If I were forced to guess, I would say that you do not play very often and rarely analyze your games, if ever."

"That would be correct, Mr. Fleischmann. To be brutally frank, I don't have the time to study and I'm not crazy for the game in the same way these guys are."

"Your honesty is refreshing. Improving your chess would be quite straightforward; it would require time and discipline. Therefore, you must consider whether, for you, the game is worth the candle."

"Now Moses." He fixed his pale blue eyes on me and I gulped; suddenly felt like I was on trial for my life. "Nothing I see here surprises me. You are an able player, very well-versed in opening play, strategically sound for the most part. But, as we have already discussed, you are habitually thwarted by your inability to concentrate. We must find a way to heal this affliction."

I couldn't think of a damned thing to say in response, so I was relieved when the door buzzer sounded, heralding the arrival of the pies, and of P.D., who must have been attracted by the irresistible aroma. (Do pizzas have pheromones?)

As we folded our slices, Viktor introduced himself and requested P.D.'s scoresheets. P.D. reached into one of the pockets of his skunky old army jacket and retrieved a fistful of paper. Oozing nonchalance, he produced a few crumpled scoresheets and tossed them on the table in front of Viktor. Borderline rude. Viktor simply smoothed out the papers and rapidly flipped through them, absorbing the games almost instantaneously. I couldn't help noticing that he gave P.D. something that none of the rest of us had got: an annotation. He'd jotted an exclamation point on one of P.D.'s sheets, chess language for a real kick-ass move.

"Mr. Morales — may I call you P.D.? It is clear that you have the mind of a chess player, but I am not certain you have the temperament. I propose to put this supposition on trial. Shall we play?"

"Not really in the mood," said P.D., impassively, between bites of pizza. This, I could tell right away, was a test. He wanted to see how Viktor would respond. I'd always envied P.D.'s special brand of cool: his sarcastic indifference, the superior, slightly hostile guard that he never dropped. Now that his passive aggression was directed toward someone I respected, it was making me cringe.

Viktor raised an eyebrow.

"Your mood, I think, is irrelevant. For the moment we will put aside consideration of your temperament. We need not connect as human beings. In cosmos of chess, we shall meet as pure, immaterial abstractions, fields of mental force interacting. You may consider us to be mere chunks of cerebral tissue floating in jars. During this game we shall have no significant physical existence. And to prove it, I will play you blindfolded. Rook odds."

He snatched the queen's rook off the board and advanced his king's pawn. Then he swiveled in his chair, turned his back to the board, and waited with arms folded. I was struck again by Viktor's flair for the dramatic; he'd created a situation in which it was pretty much impossible for his opponent to book off without looking like a wimp and a spoilsport. P.D. grinned, slipped smoothly behind the white pieces, and advanced his own king's pawn, simultaneously calling out the move.

"F3," Viktor barked. As the game progressed, he called every move instantly. It was borderline scary to watch. We'd all read about blindfold games but seeing one in person was like a magic show.

He pushed his queen's pawn, welcoming P.D. to capture it. Then things got weird. Despite having started the game five points down, Viktor continued to gamble for position, sacrificing queen's side pawns. P.D. shrugged and grabbed them. But by now white had castled and developed both bishops, which stood menacingly like machine gun nests, ready to rake fire on black's king side. P.D. tried to force a trade of queens. Viktor declined and lodged a knight deep in black territory; it was the beginning of a slick, deceptive attack that looked suicidal — until it looked murderous. The killing blow was the strangest and most elegant checkmate any of us had ever seen, with the white knight attacking the king from h8. The final position looked more like a chess problem than a real game. For a fleeting second, P.D. looked shellshocked. Then shook himself almost imperceptibly and rebooted his customary nonchalance.

"Mr. Morales, I am hoping that I have shown you that you might learn something from me. Now perhaps you will join me outside the building while I take a cigarette break. Perhaps I can teach you how to smoke *papirosi.*" He rose from his chair and unpocketed his weird Russian cigarettes. "The rest of you, please pair off as you see fit. Five minutes on the clock. I will analyze your games when I return."

We skittled till Viktor returned with P.D. The tension between them was gone; in fact, they were giving off buddy vibes. Somehow our Mister Miyagi had pulled off a miracle.

Viktor stopped by each board to check out our games, delivering rapid-fire commentary and smartly rearranging the pieces to demonstrate missed opportunities or suggest better lines. I paid close attention. I didn't know about the others, but I knew I'd learned more in a couple minutes of his analysis than I did in a hundred games of online blitz.

He returned to his seat and addressed us collectively, gesturing expansively with an unlit Russian bogey.

"My young friends, I would like to thank you. I have enjoyed myself very much. I hope that you can say the same. Not every high school student is prepared to sacrifice an hour or two keeping company with an eccentric old man."

I noticed that Viktor was no longer dropping articles. His accent was as colorful as ever, but the more he was forced to speak English, the more eloquent he became.

"If we are to continue this relationship, however, I would ask each of you to consider seriously what you want from chess. In particular, you must ask yourselves whether you aspire to achieve personal glory or to prevail as a team. I would advise you that, no matter how strong you may be as an individual, you will inevitably encounter uniquely gifted opponents to whom you must bow. I have no doubt that there are several future grandmasters competing in New York City's scholastic tournaments."

This was bitter medicine to swallow. I knew there were kids out there who were radical chess geniuses, but I hated to let go of the lurking idea that maybe someday I could ball with the best.

"What's the point, then?" Esther asked.

Viktor spread his arms in a gesture that encompassed all of us. "That is entirely up to you. I believe that you might have considerable success as a team, that together you can confront and humiliate the enemy. Who, then, is your enemy?"

After a pause, I ventured a reply.

"I can't speak for everyone else, but for me, the enemy is pretty obvious. It's those rich kids from private schools who beat us over the head with their privilege. I won't lie; I can't stand them. They treat us like we're just extras in movies they're starring in. They make us feel like we're less than nothing. Just once, I wanna to ruin their day." I looked around the room and saw my teammates nodding in agreement.

"This, I think, is possible," Viktor said. "You have identified what we may call the class enemy — pun is intended. Once you know your adversary it becomes possible to detect his weaknesses and exploit them."

"So how do we do it?" Esther asked. "Maybe P.D. and Zamir are bona fide chess wizards, but the rest of us are pretty basic."

"On the contrary," Viktor said, "each of you has the potential to become a very strong player on the scholastic level, and perhaps beyond. This does not require genius but discipline, study, and sound strategy. But what I would wish to teach you is even more important: that you can win as a team by adopting a collective approach."

Viktor reached for a cigarette, flourished a silver lighter, then remembered that he was in a school building. He sighed tragically and continued.

"In Cold War time, Soviet chess was so far superior to every other country that the capitalist bloc could only observe our supremacy with envy and awe. Perhaps you have wondered why this was so."

We all nodded, intrigued.

"Western journalists used to pester me to reveal the "secret" of Soviet chess. Because Botvinnik was a computer scientist, there were some who believed that he must have invented an algorithm for victory that was top-secret classified information, to be shared only with the strongest Soviet players. There were others who thought we had somehow rigged the entire structure of international chess competition to give our grandmasters an unfair advantage."

"There was, of course, no secret as such. But there was a way of living and of seeing the world that was unique to us. The great Botvinnik said — I am translating loosely as I speak — 'chess, like any creative activity, can exist only through the combined efforts of those who have creative talent and the ability to organize their creative work.' This was Communist thinking. We were different from you in everything we did and thought. Allow me to illustrate: You in the West would look at a great painting from the Renaissance and imagine a lone romantic genius, starving in a garret perhaps. We would look at the same painting and see the combined efforts of a team. In your movie about Michelangelo — what was it called?"

I knew this one: "*The Agony and the Ecstasy*."

"Thank you, Moses. So: In this movie the painter is shown decorating the

Sistine chapel all by himself, bickering with the pope in order to defend his personal, heroic artistic vision. In fact, the Sistine ceiling was produced by a collective, seven workers who functioned as a team under Michelangelo's guidance. This is not even counting the people who built their scaffolds, supplied their pigments, did their laundry, brought them lunch. For us, chess was no different. Our masterpieces over the board were triumphs of the whole people."

"Wait a second," Esther said. "The USSR wasn't exactly shy about promoting its individual stars. I thought the Soviet GMs were rewarded bigtime for individual achievement, just like the Olympic athletes or Yuri Gagarin. The winners got all the goodies and privileges, first-class all the way, while the people ate cabbage in shithole apartments. I figure there must have been a People's Palace of Chess with fancy offices and, I dunno, Jacuzzis and wet bars. You had to win to get the perkies, right? Otherwise, boom: off to the gulag."

"Alas, Esther, the blandishments were modest, and in my day the gulag was reserved for criminals of truly prodigious malevolence. To be sure, a few of the top players received a stipend from the state; the rest of us had to work. I was a high school English teacher for most of my career, and I confess that I have eaten plenty of cabbage. The closest I ever came to luxury was when I stayed in European hotels during international tournaments. But there was very little time for Jacuzzis and highballs; when we were not playing, we were analyzing."

"But you are nevertheless quite right," he continued, "that our greatest artists, athletes, and chess players were enthusiastically celebrated. Botvinnik even appeared on a postage stamp. But what you must understand is that for us, the achievements of any single man or woman *were* collective achievements. The excellence of Gagarin or Karpov both reflected and embodied the excellence of the socialist state, to which every one of us contributed. When they triumphed, we all triumphed."

"So how is all this going to help *us* win?" I asked, trying to cut to the chase.

"In order to explain, and at the risk of boring you all even further, perhaps I may tell you a little bit about myself. I will endeavor to keep my story brief as I am badly in need of another cigarette."

What follows is more or less what Viktor told us, as faithfully reproduced by the razor-sharp memory of Moses Middleton, Boy Genius and vocab vacuum.

7. VIKTOR'S STORY

When I was a child, the Soviet Union was a paradise for chess. Everyone played. Workers ate their lunches over the board in factory cafeterias. Little old ladies in babushkas carried pocket sets in their aprons. Every trade union had its own club, team, stars, and cutthroat rivalries. People queued at newsstands when the new issue of *Chess in the USSR* arrived.

I grew up in Krasnoyarsk, a beautiful city in Siberia with many universities and research institutions. My parents were both schoolteachers; my father was mad for chess. Once we needed to call a plumber to fix a leaky pipe in our apartment. As this plumber bent down to investigate the situation under our kitchen sink, my father noticed a rolled-up copy of *64*, the leading chess magazine, in his back pocket. My father proceeded to solicit his views on the fierce, erratic attacking style of Mikhail Tal, who had just won the world championship. A heated argument ensued. They set up a board on the kitchen table and the two were soon completely absorbed in analyzing Tal's recent games. Vodka was produced and consumed. When my mother arrived with the shopping, she was furious to discover her husband and his new comrade drunkenly singing patriotic ballads over the chessboard, as water continued to trickle onto the kitchen floor. For good and ill, this was our life, our culture.

It is neither a boast nor an exaggeration to say that the Soviets were the best. We were *by far* the best. The USSR dominated every international tournament for decades. From 1948 until the end, every world champion was one of us. (Forgive me if I omit an anomalous three-year interruption beginning in 1972, when my erratic colleague Boris Spassky became unhinged by your Bobby Fischer's psychological gamesmanship and collapsed into a quivering heap of regrets.)

There was comprehensive state support for chess, including rigorous training for all who qualified. I'm sure you all know something about Lenin:

He loved chess and did everything possible to foster it as a national sport. He valued the analytical skills and steely perseverance required by the game. Chess, he thought, would help to create the New Soviet Man — and Woman. Our superiority in chess was a matter of great national pride; we were convinced that it was evidence of the triumph of communist discipline over capitalist decadence.

Perhaps this seems naïve or silly to you. You Americans are of course far more sophisticated than we were, because you do not believe in anything. During my years in the US, I have learned that commitment, faith, and even hope, are "uncool." So I must apologize to you all, because I fear that I remain uncool. Irredeemably so.

My father taught me the game when I was perhaps six years old; within a few months I was a stronger player than he was. He took me to play at the local labor chess club, where workingmen from the factories relaxed after hours with a *kvass* and a smoke. I became their mascot. Some of these men were very strong tactical players, although they didn't have much leisure to study. By the time I was eight, I was able to defeat them all routinely. They were not resentful; on the contrary, they took great pride in me. They took up a collection to send me to a regional open tournament, where I finished first among the 12-and-unders. My little plaque was installed inside a trophy case in the labor hall, alongside photographs of the local hockey and football teams.

I joined the Krasnoyarsk Young Pioneers — a Communist version of your Boy Scouts, but for girls as well — because they sponsored a powerful chess circle. We met and played in the Pioneers' Palace, a 19th Century building of exceptional grace and luxury. After the revolution, you see, the aristocrats' estates were seized by the people and their majestic mansions were converted into centers for youth.

Training was strict and demanding: One exceptionally ruthless coach demanded that we study every one of our games for a period of 12 hours. No one actually did this, of course, but we learned much by pretending: We were forced to invent analytical shortcuts that would subsequently help our thinking over the board. The coaching was essential but the most valuable teaching and learning took place among ourselves. We played and studied as a team, analyzing each other's games and developing strategies for success in tournaments. We exercised together, sang together, socialized together; had we been adults we would doubtless have been drinking together as well.

There were no Elo ratings then, but our tournament results were published, and so our relative strengths became known to the chess establishment. At 12, I won the Krasnoyarsk Pioneer championship with a score of 15-0. I was invited to participate in national junior tournaments and progressed rapidly.

Meanwhile, I studied English literature, to which I was first attracted because I loved Sherlock Holmes, but this was a great disappointment to my father, an enthusiastic party member who wanted me to do engineering or science so as to help build the motherland. I told him that I intended to use my English to become a diplomat or a spy, and this seemed to satisfy him.

When I turned 18, I was drafted into the Red Army and stationed at Novosibirsk, the most important city in Siberia, which is not all ice and snow and desolate wastes. It was a center for physics and military research; it also had more than adequate ballet and opera.

I was not expected to act like a soldier. Only once, during basic training, did I have the opportunity to handle a Kalashnikov. I had to wear a uniform and simulate a military bearing at occasional parades; apart from that, my duty was to study, teach, and play chess for the Red Army team.

After a few months the opportunity arose to compete in the World Junior Championship, which was to be played, if I remember correctly, in Barcelona. I was eager to go, not just because the thought of spending a week in Spain appealed to my romantic sensibilities, but also because a strong showing in the Juniors would earn me a grandmaster norm.

Unfortunately, the team Army championship was to take place in Riga at exactly the same time. My colonel, who was a strict but decent sort of fellow, approached me and urged me to forego beautiful Barcelona and play instead for the honor of the Siberian Military District.

I asked him whether this was an order. He told me that I was permitted to choose, but that my choice would carry consequences. He unrolled from the ceiling an enormous map of the Soviet Union.

"This, Private Fleischmann, is our great Soviet motherland. Not long ago 20 million died to defend it from fascism."

With his stick he drew a rough circle around the eastern portion of the map.

"This, Private, is the Siberian Military District. It is home to the Eighth Army, which in 1943 lost 90,000 young men very much like you in a heroic attempt to break the siege of Leningrad."

Then he pointed to a tiny island in the Arctic Circle, on the extreme eastern border.

"What you see here, Private, is an outpost of great military significance, as it allows us to monitor the movements and signals of the Americans. It is also a part of the Siberian Military District. It is not sunny Barcelona; it is not even Novosibirsk. There is no ballet here. There is no opera here. There is nothing but a collection of huts battered by icy winds all year round. The men who serve here are heroes, but they are not happy in any sense that is familiar to you."

"Should you decide to compete in the Junior championships, I will personally make certain that you are afforded the opportunity to join these heroes for the remainder of your time in uniform. Should you choose instead to play for Siberia in the Army team championships, you will be welcome to stay in Novosibirsk, where the people of the Soviet Union provide you with healthy food, satisfactory shelter, and the leisure to pursue the great sport of chess."

He dropped his military bearing for a moment and laid an arm across my shoulder.

"This is what I would like you to understand, *malchik moi*: It is the sacrifices made by the soldiers freezing on that tiny island that permit you to devote yourself to chess in peace and comfort."

I was vexed to say the least, but I took his point. You see, we did indeed enjoy privileges, but we had to earn them. Individual achievements were honored, yes, but with the understanding that our victories reflected the collective energies and labor of the whole Soviet people. We owed them a debt.

Perhaps you see this story as an example of Communist ruthlessness. I remember it as an essential step in my maturation as a human being. Thereafter I tried to suppress my personal ambitions. This is of course very difficult for egotistical creatures like us chess players, for whom the whole world sometimes seems to exist within the boundaries of a checkered board.

Chastened, I agreed to play for Siberia and had a very strong tournament. We won; my colonel was pleased. The following year I was again invited to the Juniors, which took place in Stockholm. This time I was permitted to go. The overall winner was a young man of shocking brilliance called Anatoly Karpov, a product of the Botvinnik chess school, but I finished well enough to earn my GM norm.

After being discharged from the army, I attended university in Leningrad, where I obtained an advanced degree in English literature. My particular interest was in American authors of a Communist bent; my dissertation was on Langston Hughes. At one point I received a visit from an almost disturbingly genial apparatchik who was undoubtedly a KGB officer. (People who were perhaps overly interested in American culture tended to be investigated.) He opened a bottle of vodka and we spent an evening discussing literature, politics, and chess. Evidently he concluded that I was politically sound, because I never heard from the KGB again, not even after Korchnoi's scandalous defection. At the same time, he must have decided that I had no aptitude for spying, so one of my father's dreams fell by the wayside.

However, my father took pride and a keen interest in my chess career. I accumulated norms rapidly and became a FIDE grandmaster at the age of 23. The high school where I taught was happy to accommodate periodic absences for tournaments; I coached the student teams, and my international success was considered to reflect well on the school. I married a lovely young woman, also a schoolteacher, but the marriage did not last long. It is unfortunately true that I paid more attention to chess than I did to her. We parted amicably; there were no children.

In 1970 I took another hard lesson in humility. The most important event of the year was a political spectacle in Belgrade called "USSR vs. The Rest of the World." The tournament would be structured in such a way that each of us would play four games against one opponent from a non-Soviet country. The opposing players had been chosen according to FIDE ranking — the Elo system had only just been adopted — and they were assigned boards in order of strength. I was given the tenth and last board for the USSR team and felt affronted. I had just finished fifth in the Soviet championship, winning games against some of the world's best players. I believed that I was entitled to our fifth board.

In high dudgeon I travelled to Moscow to set forth my case. I met with Botvinnik, the patriarch of Soviet chess, who occupied a surprisingly modest little office in the People's Commissariat for Power Stations. I am ashamed to admit that I complained bitterly and at some length. Botvinnik had the mild, scholarly demeanor of a university professor, so his response was startling.

"Comrade Fleischmann: Is your hate pure?"

I was taken aback and stammered some incoherent reply. He then fixed on me the same baleful stare with which he had intimidated two generations of opponents.

"Allow me to quote Lenin: 'We are surrounded on all sides by enemies, and we have to advance almost constantly under their fire. We have combined, by a freely adopted decision, for the purpose of fighting the enemy.' This applies to the Soviet chess team as much as it does to our men in arms. When you play for the USSR, you are at war. You must hate the enemy."

"But I advise you that your hatred must be pure. It is not that you must hate any individual Western grandmaster — not even Robert Fischer — but you must hate the class and the system that we are struggling to overcome. The propaganda war is critical to our success. A tournament victory is a propaganda victory. A defeat undermines the prestige of the revolution."

He reached for a sizeable stack of computer printouts and unfolded a few pages on his desk. (As the world later learned, he had written a program that enabled him to project tournament results based on pairings.)

"Comrade Fleischmann, this tournament will not be as easy for us as the journalists seem to expect. Larsen has an unorthodox style that makes trouble for us. Portisch is very able in positional play." He smiled thinly. "I understand they call him the 'Hungarian Botvinnik'. Our fickle comrades from Czechoslovakia and Yugoslavia are stronger than we care to admit. Most importantly, Fischer is playing. You know his brilliance. At his best he is quite capable of winning all four of his games."

"Should we become complacent, should we believe too fervently in the myth of our own invincibility, we will lose." His voice became momentarily steely. "Under no circumstances will I allow that to happen."

He informed me that I would play the tenth board because I would thus be pitted against Borislav Ivkov, a Yugoslavian GM now forgotten but sometimes capable of great brilliance.

"I know your games and your tournament record. You have bested Ivkov consistently. The Americans would say that you 'have his number.' Therefore, we have made certain that you will be matched against him, an opponent against whom you will be expected to win."

Now he spoke slowly, in a quietly neutral tone that somehow exuded menace: "From you, comrade, three points are required."

"I will do my best," I replied, shaken. To score three, I would need to win both my games with white, a daunting challenge at this level of chess.

"Yes." A long pause. "You *will* do your best."

I rose, shook his hand, and turned toward the door, wondering whether my vanity had just destroyed my career. But he called me back for a final word.

"Before you go, comrade, there is something I feel I must clarify. I have spoken of hatred. Now permit me to speak of love. We Soviets place such high value on toughness that we sometimes overlook the things that give life its sweetness."

This was, I think, his way of apologizing.

"You must know you that you will not be playing for yourself. You will be playing for the Motherland and for Communism. You will be playing for every child who has pinned your photo to his bedroom wall and studies your games on his pocket set. You will be playing for the Soviet workers whose arduous labor is vindicated by our international success."

He gestured toward the wall behind him where, among various awards and memorabilia, pride of place was given to the famous photograph of Che Guevara, cigar in hand, contemplating a complex position at the Havana Olympiad.

"I do not exaggerate if I say that you are playing for our comrades everywhere in the world: for the fighters in Palestine and Mozambique, for the political prisoners in Greece, for every Vietnamese mother who has lost a son in the struggle against imperialism. Our victories, our prestige, give them hope and heart. The people love you because you represent their dream of a better world. You must love them in return."

He poured us a couple of vodkas, which we drank *na pososhok* — for the road. I left, thinking myself a better man and a true Communist. Doubtless you find all this quaint, a sentimental pep talk from a fading champion. But to me, it was deeply inspiring. I was young. I believed.

In the tournament I opened with black and managed a draw; then won with white and drew once more with black. Thus I needed a victory in the final game to secure my three points.

You will have noticed that a complex position is often reached in the middle game that seems balanced, but precariously balanced, ready to collapse into a draw unless one of the players finds an aggressive solution to the impasse. I had reached this point with Ivkov and spent 30 minutes in contemplation of my next move. I fell into a sort of swoon, haunted and harassed by the billions for whom I must win. The pressure was extreme; I could not fail them. Did I for a moment sense the presence of Che's soul gazing over my shoulder? Perhaps. At any rate, I suddenly experienced an involuntary flash of insight and read the position in an entirely new light. A line of attack was revealed to me.

Suffice it to say, I won. And my three points proved critical, just as Botvinnik had predicted. The USSR eked out a grueling one-point victory. Our top seeds, notably Spassky, did badly; we made up the necessary ground by dominating the lower boards. We all drank together that night and I raised a toast to the spirit of Che Guevara.

Resentful capitalists grumbled that we had gamed the tournament by manipulating the seeds. Why, yes: That is exactly what we did. You may be familiar with Bobby Fischer's tiresome accusations that we 'cheated' in international play. His argument amounted to the banal observation that we were more likely to agree to a quick draw in games with teammates than in games against foreign players. This was of course true; I can't deny it. It was done to conserve energy for the pairings on which the overall tournament result would depend. Is that cheating? If you like. To my mind, however, this is simply the essence of team play. It is no different than your American football teams resting their best players in meaningless games.

I make no apologies for our strategies or my beliefs. I played for another 20 years, never touching the Olympian heights of chess but deriving considerable satisfaction from individual and team victories. I coached talented young players and published a book on middle-game planning that was well received, though never translated. As the skills of my generation faded, stronger players emerged, especially the young Kasparov. The Soviet Union's superiority in chess remained unbroken through the 1980s. What broke, as you know, was the Soviet Union itself.

Our chess paradise evaporated in a frenzy of ruthless materialism. We lost everything and gained nothing, except a gleaming McDonald's restaurant in the center of Moscow.

I still grieve. Perhaps poor Spassky said it best: "If only I knew what was going to happen to our country, I would've joined the Communist Party."

8. CONSONANCES OF MELANCHOLY

Well, that was unexpected. I had thought I was introducing my teammates to Mister Miyagi; instead, we got Comrade Stalin rolling in on a Red Army tank. Everyone looked a little stunned.

Maggie broke the silence. "We're all Americans, more or less. You don't hate us, do you, Mr. Fleischmann?"

Viktor chuckled. "Of course not, my dear. I feel as Botvinnik did. I hate the American system, not the people who must contend with its injustices. I will concede, however, that the discovery of mega-meat pizza has enhanced my respect for this country."

"Surely you're not saying we need to be Communists in order to win?" Esther asked.

"No, not in the strict sense. However, I am confident that the team would improve markedly should you learn to unite against a common enemy, making use of mutual aspirations and collective effort. You needn't share my political convictions as they apply to the world at large, but you could go far together if you were to emulate the USSR over the board."

"So would you help us, Mr. Fleischmann?" Zamir asked.

"I am willing, provided that you are willing to help each other. Talk among yourselves and let me know if you would like to proceed. I would require a serious commitment from each and all of you."

This was beginning to sound a lot like my mom's "learning community." I glanced around the room.

"Is everyone up for this? Because I'm stoked." I detected various expressions of assent, ranging from goggle-eyed enthusiasm (Zamir) to wary acceptance (P.D.). Maggie looked positively dreamy, staring into the middle distance with a Mona Lisa smile. She'd been swept away by Viktor's charisma.

Now I had a proposal to float.

"Guys, a week from Saturday is Queens Chess Day. There's a tournament at Q150 in Sunnyside. Let's sign up. We'll have enough time for another training session before we play. Would that be okay, Mr. Fleischmann?"

Viktor surveyed the room coolly. "Yes, but on the following conditions." He counted off briskly with his fingers as he spoke.

"First, each of you must acquire Alexander Kotov's *The Soviet Chess School.* If it is not available in the library, you can easily find it free of charge on the Internet. This is now your Bible. I have attempted to convey something of the spirit of Soviet chess; this manual will teach you our style. Please read and play through the chapter about Botvinnik before next week."

I groaned. "That sounds a lot like homework."

"Indeed. You cannot learn properly by playing endless games of online speed chess. You must begin to study with intent. Second, you must each learn two openings, one for white and one for black: the Danish Gambit and the Scandinavian Defense. Study the main lines. Both these openings are fundamentally unsound but potentially quite powerful; I will explain what I have in mind when we reassemble."

"Third, the five of you must do something together. It might be a movie; it might be a game of basketball; it might be dinner at one of your fast-food restaurants. The choice of activity is unimportant. What is essential is that you begin to think of yourselves as a team in all aspects of your lives. Actual human contact is paramount. Communicating on your little telephones will not suffice."

"It's not going to be easy to find something we all want to do," Maggie said. "The five of us are very different people."

"That is precisely the point. You must try to create bonds that transcend your individual tastes and appetites."

We didn't have a lot of time to put this all together, so I proposed a group chat for Friday night. Pending our F2F gathering, we could hash all this out online. Now I had to ask an essential but delicate question. "What about your payment?"

"As it happens, I have already spoken to your mother about that. She will explain."

The janitor poked his head in the room and shot me a meaningful look. The building was about to close; it was time to pack up. We gathered stacks of greasy pizza boxes and prepared to go our separate ways.

As I was about to round the corner towards home, Viktor called me back.

"Moses, I have something to give you. Let us call it a talisman."

He produced a tarnished old coin, about the size and weight of a US dollar, and pressed it into my palm.

"This is a ruble from the USSR. You will note that the profile of our friend Pushkin is engraved on its face. I suggest you bring it with you to your tournaments. It is my hope that it will remind you to concentrate, much as my cigarette case has done for me."

I felt myself grinning like a fool and mumbled a thanks; for a moment I believed I was someone very special in this screwed-up world. All the way home I felt the coin's weight in my pocket and hoped it would bring me some magic.

Later that night I texted P.D., hoping to take his temperature.

>*What did u think of Viktor?*

>*Pretty sure smoking with a kid carries the death penalty in NY. The man simply does not GAF.*

>*What did he say 2U?*

> *Not much. Didn't try to be my buddy or my boss. Just showed me how that outrageous cig works. He passed the test.*

> *Relieved I am, young padawan.*

> *Don't kid yourself that I'm buying the Bolshevik Mind Magick, Comrade Middleton. But I like the guy.*

After powering through some homework, I found a free PDF of the Kotov book online, just as Viktor had promised, and dived in. Started playing through the Botvinnik games, paying close attention to the annotations. The man was a bulldozer, sweeping methodically through everything in his path and closing games with the instincts of a stone killer. Damned if I wasn't pulled into The Zone for a while; at least it felt that way. When I next noticed the clock, I saw that three hours had passed in a flash; it was 1:00 a.m. and definitely time for bed if I didn't want to be snoozing through class tomorrow morning.

You would of course despise me if I told you that I slipped the Pushkin ruble under my pillow. So let's pretend it didn't happen.

On Friday I whipped through my classes, powered by a forbidden Double-Shot Super Mocha Latte. Sprinted home, rushed through dinner, logged on for the video chat. As usual, I obsessed about choosing my avatar. Ended up rejecting a screengrab of Volonté romancing a massive spliff in *For a Few Dollars More*; instead I went with the photo of Che kibitzing in Havana, the one that Viktor had mentioned. I was happy with my choice, but I couldn't help wondering why my online brand was so important to me. Weird: I was beginning to question things I'd always done without much thought. Maybe the Viktor Virus was starting to work inside my brain.

Zamir popped into the chat room. By now he was all wired up at home and ready to rock. He hadn't figured out the avatar thing yet, so I could see his surroundings. Soccer posters on the wall. I recognized Klaus Gjasula, the Albanian midfielder who's called The Gladiator because of the Roman-looking helmet he always wears. Soccer fandom was a good sign, I thought. The whole neighborhood was mad for *fútbol*; things would get positively deranged during the Copa América with beer-soaked fans thronging the sports bars and spilling out into the street waving national flags. Maybe Zamir could become a Colombia fan; he'd fit right in. Meanwhile, though, I was going to have to introduce him to baseball. Just a month to go till Pitchers and Catchers.

"*Përshëndetje*, dude." I'd googled "hello" in Albanian.

Zamir grinned. "Whazzup, bro?" He was making a valiant effort to sound Murican but wasn't quite there yet.

P.D.'s avatar flickered into view. He was sporting an intentionally disturbing image as usual. Sometimes he was a leering Jack Nicholson from *The Shining*, sometimes a blood-spattered Christian Bale from *American Psycho*. Tonight's choice was a nightmarish modernist painting of what appeared to be a ghoulish priest surrounded by hanging beef carcasses.

"P.D., what the hell *is* that?"

"Francis Bacon, *Figure with Meat*. It's here for your edification, Mose, since your knowledge of 20th Century figurative painters strikes me as deficient. If you pay real close attention, you'll see it in the original *Batman* flick, one of the lame ones with Michael Keaton — more your speed."

Moments later Maggie materialized behind a *kawaii* cartoon face; then arrived Esther, who was — of course — Joseph Bologne, Chevalier de Saint-Georges.

Arrayed on the *Brady Bunch* grid, we joked around for a few minutes, making sport of various teachers, celebs and ninth-grade jamokes. But something about our virtual faces wasn't sitting right with me.

We hid behind avatars for various reasons. The illusion of privacy was a big one. It's amazing how much you can learn about people by scoping out their rooms in video chat; it's a little creepy when you think about it. With an avatar nobody sees your piles of dirty laundry or reads the titles of the books on your wall. No one knows if you live in a shithole rental, sharing a bedroom with your siblings because your family can't afford the space. You feel free in cyberspace; you're judged only on whatever floating identity you choose to construct. You can chat while freeballing, if that's your thing, and nobody's the wiser.

As for me, I had to admit, a big part of it was trying to make an impression online. I wanted to project a cool personal brand, and I usually did it by piggybacking on somebody else's image: Volonté, Che, Muhammad Ali, Miles Davis, whoever. Tonight, though, the emptiness of my branding gestures was hitting me hard for the first time. It was pathetic, really: Why was I thinking that some colorful arrangement of pixels, no matter how lovingly curated, was going to enhance my dubious image? Screw it, I thought, and switched off the avatar. My own face appeared. It was what it was; I ain't no movie star.

"Could that be the real Moses Middleton on display?" exclaimed P.D. "You beautiful beast. At this late hour I would have expected you to be wearing your superhero jammies."

Heading off an inevitable series of Moses jokes, I jumped in and did my moderator thing.

"Esteemed teammates: Can I ask you all a favor? This will seem weird, but I think we should all be able to see each other. It would feel like a step closer to reality. I guess I'm remembering what Viktor said about the need for human connection. Hide your backgrounds if you want, but let's make some eye contact here."

To my astonishment, everyone complied, even P.D. The Viktor Virus was spreading. Maybe we were all changing just a little, hopefully for the better.

"So, comrades, is everyone up for the Fleischmann Plan?"

I heard grunts of assent; saw nods. Esther broke in.

"Let's put it this way. I'll go along, but provisionally. Let's follow the program, meet with Viktor next week, then give the tournament a shot. If we do well, then yeah, I'm in. Otherwise, I'll need to reconsider. I have a lot on my plate."

"What about that thing we all have to do together? Any ideas?"

"On this issue, boys and girls, no discussion is necessary," Esther pronounced. "Here's the deal: Tomorrow night I'm playing in a concert at St. Marks Church. The program is baroque chamber music. Every one of you *needs* to be there. If I'm expected to spend my valuable time chasing chess glory, it's the least you can all do."

Apart from Esther, none of us was into classical music, but nobody was going to risk her wrath. It was a done deal the moment she proposed it.

"Formal dress required?" I asked, dreading the answer. The closest thing I had to dress-up was a bargain-basement suit left over from my Middle School moving-up ceremony. It made me look like an inner-city dork in hand-me-downs.

"Only for me, Mose. The rest of you can show up in flip-flops and weed T-shirts as far as I'm concerned."

"Pity," P.D. said. "I so rarely have the opportunity to don my spats and white waistcoat."

"Cut the crap, P.D: Just make sure your ass is in the seat," Esther said, a little threateningly. "You'll all be on the comp list. I'll be taking names." She texted us the time and place; chat over.

As faces winked out, Zamir shot me a private message; asked me to hang in for a minute.

"Mose, there is something I think we should do. As a team. In my country, after a performance we give the lady a bouquet of roses."

"We do that here, too," I said, remembering the time my dad dragged me to the Metropolitan Opera to hear Anna Netrebko, his favorite. She brought down the house and was more or less pelted with bouquets.

"I think we should do this for Esther. There is a problem, though. I checked at the flower shop and it will cost $40. I only have $5 right now."

I pondered the situation for a moment. "It's a great idea, Zamir. I bet I can scrounge up ten bucks. Then I'll see what I can get from P.D. and Maggie. If we fall short, I can pretty much guarantee that my parents will make up the difference. This is just the kind of thing that gets them amped up."

"I think perhaps Viktor would approve," Zamir said with a sly grin. "As a wise man said: From each according to his ability; to each according to his need."

Was this irony? Maybe there was more to my Balkan sidekick than met the eye.

Shutting the laptop, I hastened my ass through the house looking for Mom, eager to raise various financial issues but also to clue her in on my latest YouTube find, *Hercules and the Conquest of Atlantis*. No Steeve Reeves in this one, but it starred an equally inept mound of muscles named Reg Park, along with the usual complement of tunic-wearing ruffians swilling wine and kicking the crap out of each other. Best of all, appearing in a bit part as the sneering king of Sparta, was Gian Maria Volonté, dressed casket sharp in an outrageously inauthentic costume that looked like a leather miniskirt. I was jazzed; this was like finding out that the butler in your favorite craptacular sitcom was played by Laurence Olivier.

Mom was up for it. We grabbed our usual places on the sofa and I booted up the tube. Allegra drifted in with Julian and they settled down to watch with us. For Allegra it was a nostalgia trip. Turned out she'd seen some of the Herc flicks dubbed into Spanish when she was a kid; even in Italian she could more or less follow the dialogue. (TBH, these movies could have been dubbed in Elvish and any idiot could've grasped the plot; subtlety was not one of their strong points.) She promised to introduce me to *Lucha Libre* films, which evidently involved masked wrestlers running around Mexico brawling with crooks, monsters and mad scientists. Right up my alley. Meanwhile, I couldn't help noticing that she and Julian were looking pretty cozy together. Maybe something romantic was in the works; if so, it wouldn't be the first time love had blossomed in the hectic halls of Hotel Middleton.

The film opened with a 10-minute gang beatdown in an Ancient Greek cantina and closed with the apocalyptic destruction of Atlantis. (Surprisingly decent FX for a Herc flick.) In between, my man faced down various monsters and a squadron of identical Aryan-looking stormtroopers. My dad, who was half-watching as he processed email on a laptop, remarked that the flick could be read as a metaphorical treatment of Italy's struggle against the Nazis. I begged him not to ruin it by overthinking, though I could see that he was probably right. As the sun set over the Aegean, signifying the end of another Herculean escapade, I had my chance to check with Mom about money. I was relieved to hear that Viktor's compensation was done and dusted.

"He and I made a barter arrangement," Mom explained. "He's going to give your club an hour of his time every week; in exchange, he gets an hour of my time. Works out nicely for all parties. In fact, you might say Viktor is getting a BOGO deal, because those coaching sessions will be therapeutic for him." She grinned. "As long as you kids don't drive him crazy, that is."

As for the flowers, Mom was more than agreeable. She and Dad would make up the difference so long as everybody contributed a little piece, whatever they could afford. She was proud of me, she said; I was showing emotional maturity and all kinds of other good stuff that psychotherapists rate highly. Embarrassing, yeah, but nice.

Back in my room, I got online and collected virtual cheddar from Maggie and P.D.; Mom topped me up and I pushed the money to Zamir via cash app. Spent the rest of the evening learning the Danish Gambit and the Scandinavian Defense, two super-aggressive openings where you sacrifice a center pawn right out of the gate. Wild; looked the kind of thing Magnus Carlsen would play in a blitz game.

The next day, Saturday, raced by. I ran the Danish and Scandinavian a few times in an online speed room; to my surprise, I won all the games. Both openings seemed to have an unsettling effect on opponents. I thought I was beginning to see what Viktor had in mind.

A little before eight o'clock that evening, everyone — except Esther, of course — gathered in front of the church, where the notice board announced a concert by something called the Queens Baroque Ensemble. Zamir brought the flowers, awkwardly but effectively concealed in a giant-sized Rite Aid shopping bag. We greeted each other a little uncertainly and entered the nave. We slid into a pew side-by-side — close to the front, so Esther couldn't miss us — and riffled through our programs. None of the music was familiar to me and I steeled myself for a long, boring evening.

Lights dimmed; candles were lit. Eight musicians walked on stage carrying various stringed instruments, some of them familiar — violins and cellos — as well as weird surprises, like some gargantuan lute-looking thing with a neck that had to be three feet long. (After consulting the program, I figured it had to be a "theorbo," a genuinely danky word but not one that I expect to see on the SATs).

Among the performers were a couple of beardo guys in black turtlenecks, but it was mostly women, and they were all styling the kind of formal dresses you usually only see in magazines. The sight was impressive, but there could be no doubt that every eye in the hall was riveted on Esther, who glided on stage, lean, lofty and regal in a shimmering floor-length red gown. I was stupefied. I'd never seen her in anything but tees and leggings. But here she was, tight, sassy and red-carpet ready.

"Holy hell, where did she get that dress?" I whispered to Maggie.

"Some special program she's tapped into; rich ladies donate last year's couture to deserving young musicians. She looks awesome, right?"

"Awesome is understating it. She looks like Queen Nzingha of Ndongo."

I didn't know much about baroque music, so I wasn't sure what to expect. To my ear, Bach and Vivaldi had always sounded like a room full of sewing machines next door. Esther and the theorbo guy moved to the front. He laid down a strumming beat and Esther began to play. It was sweet soulful melody that gave me a little flutter inside; no sewing machines in the house. I checked the program: "False Consonances of Melancholy," whatever that meant, by some dude called Nicola Matteis. I settled back in my chair. This was going to be okay.

As the evening progressed I checked out my teammates, trying to gauge their reaction. Zamir and Maggie looked rapt, grooving with eyes closed. P.D. was unreadable as usual, but I thought I could detect a slight oscillation of his left foot that just might be the equivalent of tapping along. The music continued for 90 minutes or so with various configurations of instruments. Lots of composers I'd never heard of; crazy sounds ranging from soulful to in-your-face jubilant.

The one constant was Esther: Whenever she took the lead, everyone braced for something special. I eyed the muscles of her right arm flexing as she bowed the tunes, followed her long powerful fingers as they pattered up and down the neck of her softly glowing fiddle. I saw her face transformed by some beautiful, mysterious emotion that I hadn't known was inside her. Melancholy, yes — but also longing, wistfulness, maybe a touch of hope? I wondered if it was pervy to watch her so closely; decided I didn't care.

As an encore they played something I actually recognized, the infamous Pachelbel Canon. I knew it as a monotonous, droning joint that had put more people to sleep than Benadryl. But the way they played it was nothing like what I was expecting. It was quick, bouncy and light. I figured this was the way it was s*upposed* to sound before the FM deejays turned it into middle-class background music.

The applause at the end was fairly thunderous for a twee little Episcopal church in northern Queens. When Esther took a solo bow, I lost my head and yelled "*brava!*" For an agonizing second, I was sure I'd made a fool of myself, ass hanging in the wind as usual. But it turned out I was right on point: I'd broken the ice and other people joined in. I even heard a "*bravissimo*" or two. I'd figured Esther was good, but this was the first time it hit me *how* good. She might actually have a future with this music thing. Hell, she'd probably end up playing Carnegie Hall while I'd be bussing tables at the diner across the street.

"This boy is proppa poleaxed," exclaimed P.D. as the ovation died away. "I actually *enjoyed* that."

"No words," Maggie agreed, looking dreamy, while Zamir nodded vigorously.

We hung in front of the church waiting for Esther. When she appeared, she was back in her usual discount streetwear; the Cinderella dress was slung over her shoulder in a dry-cleaning bag. For once, she was all smiles; this was a rare and ravishing thing to see.

"That was a fetching frock, girl," P.D. said. "I had to scrape Mose's tongue off the floor with a spatula."

I cringed. My relationship with Esther was fraught enough as it was; the last thing I needed was her thinking I was digging her chili. She'd be on her guard all the time. I ventured a compliment.

"Esther, damn, you can really play. I'm rocked." Weak, I know: best I could do on the spur of the moment.

Esther went Full Brit. "It is happy for you that you possess the talent of flattering with delicacy." Had to be something from one of her Jane Austen shows; I suspected I'd been dissed. With delicacy.

We all did our best to make congratulations and compliments worthy of the occasion; funny how much harder it is to express honest admiration than to reel off the usual string of insincere bullshit. Then Zamir reached into his bag and produced the flowers with a flourish.

Esther actually squealed with pleasure, another first. "Zamir, you have stolen my heart." She stooped and gave him a little smooch on the cheek.

"It's from all of us," Zamir said.

"Even P.D.? Will wonders never cease? I have to say it: Thanks. Y'all made me feel like a diva. Maybe we're a team after all."

Maggie beamed; you could tell how much it thrilled her to see her BFF in a joyful mood.

"We should do something together every week," she said. "Viktor was right. It feels wonderful."

I'd just scored my weekly allowance and it was burning a hole in my pocket, so I offered to treat the gang to *alfajores* at the Uruguayan bakery up the street. (If you're so unfortunate as to live somewhere without access to Latin American goodies, you should know that these are fresh-baked sandwich cookies with dulce de leche in the middle; it's like your Golden Double Stuf died and went to heaven on wings of caramel.)

We were loping like a wolf pack toward the 37th Avenue business district, laughing and chattering, when some random dude stepped out of a doorway and parked himself directly in our path.

"Meiling!" he barked. What followed was a harsh, rapid-fire string of what I assumed was Chinese, obviously directed at Maggie. Not a random dude at all; this had to be her creepy-ass uncle. He was younger than I expected, wearing a beanie and a cheap puffy jacket. For some reason I'd been picturing a middle-aged stooprider with a Beijing Bikini. This guy was rigid, tense, radiating hostile vibes.

Maggie wilted visibly as he spoke. Her shoulders dropped and she seemed to shrink back into herself. All the evening's joy evaporated in an instant. She turned to us and muttered, "Sorry-guys-have-to-go-see-you-at-school." Creepy Uncle grabbed her upper arm and briskly steered her away down the block.

"What. The. Actual. Eff." This was P.D., sounding decidedly sinister. He turned to Esther. "Do you have the slightest clue what that was all about?"

"I'm afraid so, but I can't explain right now. There's a situation."

"I am about *this* close to running after that muffa and putting my foot up his ghastly ass."

"Hold off, P.D., please. I need to think some things through."

We could only stare as Maggie melted into the darkness. Utterly deflated, we abandoned the *alfajores* mission and scattered. A perfect evening. Shot to shit.

9. FIRST TOUCH

In the aftermath of this monumental letdown, young Moses Middleton experienced some real consonances of melancholy. I was maximally stressed that night; I could barely sleep. Brief intervals of unconsciousness were interrupted by mad dreams straight out of Dr. Freud's database, with oversized chess pieces and theorbos prominently featured. Sprang out of bed in the morning with a nervous stomach; saw that P.D. had sent me a couple of WTF texts that I would need to answer somehow.

I worked up my courage and called Esther.

She was not her usual ornery self; I could hear dejection in her voice. I congratulated her once more for owning the whole baroque era on the previous night; told her how sorry I was that her triumph was spoiled. Then I raised the P.D. issue.

"For now, just tell him that Maggie has a strict uncle who watches her like a hawk," Esther advised. "You don't need to let on that he's some kind of sexual predator. P.D. would go ballistic, and the consequences could be, shall we say, problematic."

"Fair enough. But Esther, I'm super worried about Maggie. She's too vulnerable to push back against this guy. She needs our help to get through this. I feel terrible just doing nothing."

"How the hell do you think *I* feel?" Esther snapped. "She's my best friend. This is eating me up inside."

What I needed to say now was going to piss Esther off, I was sure, but I had to try.

"You're taking on this whole dumpster fire on the solo; it's too much responsibility for a high school kid. I know we agreed to keep the situation to ourselves but this is not working for me, and I can't see how it could be working any better for you. We can't fix this alone. Would it be all right with you if I discussed this with someone? Confidentially, for sure — no names, completely hypothetical. I hate to admit it, but I need advice. From an adult."

A long pause followed by an unexpected response. "I guess. But not your mom. She'll grab you by the neck and won't let go until you spill the whole story. Then she'll leap into action and take no prisoners."

"Okay, agreed. I'll find someone else, someone I can trust. I'll get back to you if I hear anything useful."

Who could I ask? Not Viktor; this wasn't the kind of problem that existed in his world. But the advantage of living in a big, crazy house like ours is that you have a lot of options when you need somebody's help. It had to be a woman; I was savvy enough to realize that women were bound to have better insight on issues of sexual abuse and harassment. Obvi I wasn't going to burden Allegra with this — her English was spotty, and she was working though some issues of her own — so I landed on Mallika.

I lucked out that morning; when I went to the kitchen to brew up, she was already there. She agreed to chat on the down-low and suggested we go out to the nearest coffee shop, since Ritwik was sleeping off a 36-hour shift in their room. We threw on our jackets and trotted down the block to a Colombian place. (I tried to avoid the multi-national coffee behemoths when I could; I'd rather scatter my meager allowance among local businesspeople than drop it in the pocket of some mega-billionaire tycoon.) I ordered a couple of pastries and some sweet, milky coffee, swallowed hard, and got started.

"I'm going to tell you a weird story. I thought about pretending that it's all hypothetical, but that wouldn't fool anybody, least of all you. So I'll give you the 411 but I won't name names. I'm going to have to trust you to keep it between us. For now, anyway."

I ran through the whole narrative, trying to omit what the tech companies call "personally identifiable information." I was well aware that it wouldn't be too challenging to figure out who I was talking about. But once I jumped in, I felt like I had to keep swimming forward or die, like a Great White Shark. (Okay, maybe a Small Brown Shark.) Mallika looked grave but not exactly shocked; I suspected she ran into situations like this at the law clinic on the regular.

"I'm really sorry to dump this in your lap, and it makes me cringe to talk about it, but I'm totally frustrated. What the hell do I do about this creep?"

Mallika thought for a long time; I looked on as various emotions registered on her features. She had an analytical mind, and I could almost see the wheels turning. Finally she looked me straight in the eye and spoke.

"I think you may be approaching this from the wrong angle. The way I see it, the crux of this whole situation is her mother's status. If she had a green card, and a job she wasn't ashamed of, there would be no problem — or at any rate, no problem that couldn't be solved. If she could be home in the evenings, this uncle character wouldn't have much scope to mess with your friend. And even if he did, various actions could be taken without us worrying that Child Protective Services would deem her an unfit mother."

"Can we get her a real job without papers?"

"It's complicated. Technically a boss could be penalized for hiring an undocumented worker, but it almost never happens. I don't have to tell you that a pretty large percentage of the working people in this neighborhood are undocumented. This is a sanctuary city, so NYPD doesn't usually shake people down for green cards. The feds are the ones you have to worry about. When ICE goes after some local sweatshop, it's almost always for political reasons, and the process is arbitrary and often corrupt. Odds are, she could probably get a job without much risk to the employer."

Mallika sighed, sipped her coffee, and grimaced. That sugary brew is perfect for starting your heart in the morning but it can be nasty when it gets cold.

"Mose, immigration is the bureaucracy from hell. You can't count on anything these days; the rules are changing all the time. As far as the government is concerned, it's 'give us your tired, your poor' — but don't expect anything in return; at best we'll just look the other way while they do the essential work that no one else wants to do. In the long term, there are various pathways to a green card. They make allowances for immigrants in STEM fields. If she's overstayed a student visa, it could get dicey. But there's a huge backlog: It can take years to process a green card application, and that could work in her favor. If she gets a science-y job and has a visa application under review, I think the authorities would be unlikely to swoop down on her child. We should play for time. If I were to take on her case on pro bono, I think I could generate enough red tape to string this out for years. The daughter's a citizen, right? Once she's reached the age of majority, the girl could even sponsor her own mom. Meanwhile, the priority is to find her a respectable job."

"Got it. But I can't just leap in like Hercules, busting heads and trying to save the situation by brute force. To begin with, I need to get my friend on board with this."

"I agree; you can't set any of this in motion without talking to the girl first. You have to engage with her directly. You're not doing Esth— I mean, you're not doing your other friend any favors by leaving her in the middle of all this."

So Mallika had figured out who was who. What the hell; it was almost a relief. As every high school kid knows from hard experience, the elaborate circuitry of shared secrets can be murder. You can barely keep track of who knows what, let alone who is not *supposed* to know.

"The girl is reluctant to talk about this problem because she is ashamed. This is quite typical with victims of abuse. It's horrible, but they blame themselves. And you're embarrassed to intervene. You're afraid of angering her or making a fool of yourself. But Mose, this is an emergency. Her well-being is at stake. You simply must risk it. See what you can discover about her mother's qualifications; then we could think about finding a job to match. Above all, see whether the girl is in immediate danger. In that case you may be forced to blow the whistle, regardless of the consequences."

"That's what really has me worried. Even if we can fix things for her mom, it's going to take time. And meanwhile, it sounds like this creep may be right on the verge of doing something unspeakable."

"I'm going to go out on a limb and offer some advice that you wouldn't usually hear from a lawyer, or from most 'responsible adults.' If you get the slightest hint that things are about to go critical, confront him. Threaten him with consequences. The more I deal with situations like this, the more convinced I become that we need to get brutally tough with men who harass women. Call him out. It will put him on notice and hopefully buy the girl some time. Hell, take your friend P.D. with you; he'd scare anybody. No violence, needless to say. If anything happened to you, your mother would never forgive me — I would never forgive myself, for that matter. So back off immediately if the situation gets dicey. If you want, Ritwik and I can arrange to be nearby. Should things get too fraught, call us. We'll be there in a flash."

As we walked back to the homestead, I tried to make sense of conflicting advice. Esther wanted me to keep P.D. in the dark; Mallika, surprisingly, recommended unleashing his awesome powers of intimidation. In your typical Afterschool Special, the troubled kid seeks out a sympathetic adult who invariably provides coherent Received Wisdom on which he can safely act. Justice is served, happiness restored. In real life, everyone has their own idea of what should be done, and you find yourself being pushed in different directions. I would take Mallika's guidance under advisement, but there was some shit that I was just going to have to resolve for myself.

Now I had to reach out to Maggie. Over the past few days I had begun to feel as though my whole life was about wrangling far-flung yoots and arranging interlocking meetings. Moses Middleton, the Human Switchboard. Hercules Meets the Mad Facilitator. Did I have a talent for this stuff? I should be figuring out what I'm good at, I thought, so as to plan my future the way the teachers say we should. But if my unexpected flair for organizing meant becoming a gladhanding corporate events planner, I'd sooner be unemployed. I filed the issue away for future consideration and returned to the matter at hand.

This would be my second actual phone call today, which was a little odd. Like most of my friends, I rarely made a voice call. We preferred texting, or almost any form of online communication. I can't speak for the other kids, but to me, ringing people felt almost rude, as though you were expecting them to jump to attention and respond immediately. You hated it when somebody answered and sounded annoyed or sleepy. In this case, however, I had to make an exception. I would need to use persuasion to arrange facetime, and my dubious little arsenal of masculine wiles wouldn't work very well on SMS.

Maggie was not thrilled to hear from me.

"Mose, if this is about last night, I really, *really* don't want to talk about it. I'm mortified enough as it is."

I took a deep breath and launched my pitch.

"It's hard to say this without sounding like some phony on tv, but I care about you and I'm worried. I need to talk to you in person so I can try to make sense of what's going on. I've been picking up scary vibes and ignoring them, being an egotistical prick as usual. I don't want to be that way anymore. I've decided I have to stand up for my friends. But I can't do anything to help unless you let me. Come out and meet me tomorrow at noon. We'll go someplace quiet and talk. Do it for my sake. Please?"

I couldn't make puppy-dog eyes over the phone, so I had to hope the sad-animal pleading was coming through in my voice. Maggie was a sucker for anything cute or poignant.

"All right, Mose. I surrender. I think I can spare an hour. But there's a problem. This is going to sound weird, but I can't just leave the house when I want to. That guy you saw last night — he's my uncle — gives me the third degree whenever I go outside. It's crazy but it's what I live with."

"Jesus, can't you just make something up? Tell him it's my birthday and you promised to take me out for soup dumplings. Or just tell him we're in a lab together and we have to prepare a report."

My impatience must have been showing through; Maggie sounded miserable.

"Don't *you* start being mean, Mose. I couldn't stand it. Everyone's down on me all the time; you're the only boy who's ever nice to me."

Damn, I was blowing it already. I apologized for a while and eventually regained the ground I'd lost. She relented. We were on for Sunday.

***

Blam!

Zamir and I were walking across the playground, bound for snacks at the halal stand, when I was blindsided by brain-rattling blow to the head. I saw stars for a second; felt like I'd been smacked with a truncheon. I wheeled around and beheld the ugly sight of Marco and Steve, leering at me while passing around a soccer ball.

I'd arranged to hang out with Zamir that Saturday afternoon. He didn't know where my house was, so we'd met at the school. Neither of us was expecting an encounter with the Testosterone Twins.

"Nice header, Middleton," Marco sneered. "Now here's one for your girlfriend." He dropkicked the ball, hard, aiming straight for Zamir's face.

I had a very bad feeling, expecting a broken nose or a smackdown, but what happened instead was magnificent. Zamir deftly received the ball on his forehead, arrested the rebound with one hand and dumped the ball to his shoetops, where he proceeded to juggle and juke it like a hot-dogging striker. He flipped the ball upward with one toe and caught it on his fingertip, slapping it to give it the classic Globetrotter spin. Then he let it roll up his forearm and shoulder all the way up to his neck. He began to bob and weave, propelling the ball so that it whirled it around his head and shoulders. It was exceptionally kickass; I'd never seen anything like it outside of YouTube. He capped his impromptu freestyle show with a no-look header straight into Steve's chest.

"You need to work on your first touch," Zamir said. *Boom.* He stalked — did I detect a hint of swagger? — out of the playground, while Marco and Steve stared open-mouthed. There was going to be a reckoning with those two sad lads, I felt sure, but it wasn't going to happen today.

I hustled after him, wiped off the tip of my pocket mod, and proffered a congratulatory hit. He declined with a somewhat shocked expression, and explained that while everybody smoked cigarettes in Albania, vaping was strictly *verboten.* Weird country.

"Zamir, where did you learn to do that freestyling shit? It was awe-inspiring."

"In Albania everybody plays football as soon as they can walk. We say that if you pass a ball to an American, he'll catch it with his hands. If you pass a ball to an Albanian, he'll take it with his feet and juggle."

"You must be a star back in Albania."

"No, I am — how do you say? — in the middle."

"Mediocre?"

"Yes, mediocre. I am not quick enough across the field. Others are much better."

"Well, you'd be a standout here in JH, that's for sure." I told Zamir about the youth soccer leagues that played every weekend in Flushing Meadows, an enormous, somewhat shabby public park where cricket pitches and baseball diamonds could be found alongside a complex of soccer fields with tatty artificial surfaces. He wasn't interested. Right now, he said, his life was all about playing chess and mastering English in advance of the SATs. He was still a huge fan of Gjasula, as the poster on his wall suggested, but chess — which he regarded as a sport — had completely captured his imagination. A couple of years ago his dad had taken him to a simultaneous exhibition by Erald Dervishi, the only Albanian GM, and he was hooked.

Today Zamir was sporting another Albanian T-shirt, this one even more monumentally pogo than the last. It said: "Why turn down? I am fabulous!" Wanted it. Maybe I could have one just like it printed up at one of those custom trophy shops on Roosevelt Avenue.

I brought him home and we settled in the kitchen while we wolfed down our shawarmas. Various members of my hyper-extended family drifted in and out; introductions were made.

My dad, fixing himself a Dagwood from yesterday's leftovers, was intrigued by the whole Albanian thing. He asked Zamir what he thought about Viktor's communist spiel; we learned some of his life story in response. I vaguely knew that Albania had been commie till the early 90s; what I didn't know was that its supreme leader, Enver Hoxha (no relation!), believed that the USSR had betrayed the revolution after Stalin's death. Zamir's grandparents were Party stalwarts and they *hated* the Soviets; they preferred Mao. His parents, who had owned a coffee shop in Tirana, were pretty apolitical. They loved Albania but wanted Zamir to get a college degree with some kind of prestige. They heard about New York City's Albanian doorman mafia, scored a position at a Jackson Heights high-rise condo, and figured they would be able to save enough to put Zamir through one of the SUNYs. His dad worked long hours and his mom mostly stayed home, cooking Albanian delicacies that I was eager to sample. He promised to bring me something called a *byrek*, a kind of stuffed pastry that he assured me would blow my mind. As for Viktor's Marxist worldview, he could take it or leave it. It was the Soviet approach to chess, not the system of government, that interested him.

"It makes sense to me because in Albania it is still natural to do things cooperatively," he explained. "Maybe this is left over from communist days? I don't know. We have individual goals, but we believe we need to support each other to achieve them. This doorman — network?"

I nodded.

"This doorman network is an example. Albanians are always ready to help other Albanians. So I am comfortable with the idea of collective effort."

My dad nodded sagely. "Would you say that the culture of communism survives even if the system of government has collapsed?"

"A little yes, a little no. My grandparents always say that in communist time, a beautiful woman could walk alone all the way from Tirana to Saranda without fear of men doing bad things. Instead they would call her 'sister' and give her any help she needed. I do not think this is still true."

"Well, it sure as hell isn't true in New York City," my dad said, and I nodded. In Jackson Heights, my friends told me, a girl couldn't walk down the street without getting hit with relentless harassment, ranging from wolf whistles to open sexual invitations. I hoped Zamir would be able to adjust to the stark cruelty of life in the 718; it had to be weird for him.

Dad turned to me. "Mose, bring this young man over for dinner any time. Albania is bound to get the whole gang in gear. I can already hear us yelling at each other about Hoxhaism. It'll be just like Plato's *Symposium*, but with women. And without slaves."

Later Zamir and I rolled out the chessboard in the living room and played skittles while we watched YouTube on the big monitor. I wanted to see an Albanian movie, but almost nothing was available with English subtitles. We landed on an old B&W flick called *Tomka and His Friends*, about a bunch of kids who join the partisan resistance when Nazi invaders take over their soccer field. Apropos, right? Once again, it felt like various threads of my life were being woven together in some larger pattern that I couldn't yet make out. I was reminded of Esther's concert. Some of that crazy music really spoke to me, especially the ones that layered harmonies over a repeating bass line — a musical strategy not unlike some of my favorite jams — culminating in a soaring melody that pulled all the voices together into a seamless whole. Anyway, these Albanian youths turned a team sport into a collective crusade and ended up kicking Nazi ass all the way back to the Rhineland.

Speaking of ass-kicking, Zamir trounced me a few times before the movie ended and he had to leave. My boy was a monster over the board. Real life, on the other hand, could be harder to control, so I warned him to watch his back for the next few. It was inevitable that Marco and Steve would launch some kind of reprisal in order to recapture what passed for their dignity. Zamir just shrugged. He was fatalistic, one of those fortunate people who never seemed to worry about anything.

"In Albania we say: '*Ujku qimen e nderron po zakonin se harron.*' Means, the wolf can change his hairs but not his habits."

"Well, in Italian they say: '*Nessuno mi unfungulo*'." (I won't translate; all you connoisseurs of politically incorrect Mafia movies will understand.) "So raise the alarm if they mess with you."

I saw him off, hoping for the best as he sauntered blithely down the street in his proudly bogus tee.

10. THE LABORS OF MOSES MIDDLETON

Next morning I woke up anxious again, not just because I was meeting Maggie, but also because of a nagging feeling that I'd forgotten something. Once I cleared my head with a jolt of caffeine, I remembered. I needed to whip up a PowerPoint presentation on some famous Italian. The teacher wanted us to learn something about culture and history along with the language as such, which was more than cool with me. Ran it past my dad, who hopefully suggested Giuseppe Verdi, but inevitably I opted for a movie guy instead, specifically my current man crush, Gian Maria Volonté.

I flipped open the laptop and was soon sampling stills and factoids from a metric ass-ton of browser tabs. These revealed, among much else, that Volonté was a major Communist activist who used his stardom as a platform to campaign against the Vietnam War and the fascist coup in Chile. My man even smuggled a political prisoner out of Italy on his sailboat. He did radical street theater and chose his movie roles as an expression of political commitment. (That priceless Hercules gig and those spaghetti Westerns, it turns out, were just desperation moves to pay the rent when he was struggling). I spent the morning mashing together what I hoped was a balanced summary of his life and works. I foregrounded the serious films but made sure to include a clip of the immortal gun duel from *For a Few Dollars More* so my classmates wouldn't fall asleep. Final screen was a quote from the director Giuliano Montaldo, who delivered Volonté's eulogy: "*Non aveva paura di niente, ha osato tutto.*" He feared nothing; he dared everything.

It was a little disconcerting to discover that the Coolest Dude Who Ever Lived (with the obvious exception of the Chevalier de Saint-Georges) was a bigtime commie. I'd always thought of Reds as humorless bruisers in bad suits, banning books and throwing dissidents in the gulag. But the stereotype sure didn't fit Gian Maria — or Che, the rockstar revolutionary with a jones for chess. Since encountering Viktor, I was finding commies wherever I looked. It felt like I was exhuming (*vocab alert!*) a secret history, long forbidden to Americans but lurking just beneath the surface of everything, like midichlorians of radicalism. I realized that it was only lately, now that communism was no longer seen as a threat, that it seemed permissible to talk about it. Within limits you were allowed to acknowledge its bygone beauty, as though you were admiring a dead butterfly pinned to a board. Still, I sensed that I was wandering across dangerous territory and wondered if I shouldn't tread carefully lest I end up with a reputation as some kind of crazed radical, running a chess club as a front for subversive activity.

Nah, screw that. Here I was, grooming myself to ace the SATs, tweaking my personal style to accommodate the prejudices of corporate scumbags, flattering authority, sliding past conflict. If I stayed on this path, they'd be carving "In Loving Memory of a Skillful Ass Kisser" on my tombstone. Could I be more like Gian Maria? *Non aveva paura di niente, ha osato tutto.* A tall order, but I thought I'd try to remember the epitaph as I grappled with the outrageous challenges that life was now throwing in my face.

I took Maggie to one of the diners on 37th Avenue, where we both ordered the Cheeseburger Deluxe. Did some quick calculations and decided to spring for it. Picking up two tabs in two days was going to kill what was left of my allowance; trying to solve the world's problems will cost you. She wouldn't look at me while we waited for the food; her eyes were cast downward to the cheaply printed paper placemat, where she was half-consciously defacing thumbnail portraits of 45 U.S. Presidents with her Hello Kitty ballpoint, paying special attention to Donald Trump: horns, fangs, the works. She looked like she was experiencing what I always felt in the doctor's waiting room, when I would try to buck myself up for the ordeal to come by promising myself it would soon be over. I had to break the silence.

"Maggie, I —. You —." I trailed off, completely at a loss.

At last she looked up and made eye contact. Her fathomless brown eyes were borderline teary but she managed an ironic smile. "Moses, you look so woebegone I could almost think you're feeling worse than I do. I'm going to take pity on you and give you the whole story."

It all came tumbling out. Her mom and dad had come to the U.S. 15 years earlier on student visas. When the visas expired, they overstayed, figuring they could fix the immigration issues once they were established. Their idea was to start a business, one of those trinket shops on Roosevelt Avenue. They couldn't get a small biz loan without green cards, so they had to borrow from the neighborhood sharks. These guys weren't Mafia-style extortionists but local Chinese-American businessmen supporting their community; they charged more interest than a bank would, but the vig was borderline manageable for a hardworking family.

When Maggie was born, her mom could no longer put in the necessary hours at the store. Her dad brought his brother, Chen, over from China to stock the shelves and work the register. Everybody had to bust their asses, in the great tradition of Queens immigrants, but things seemed to be working out reasonably well — until her dad died suddenly of some mysterious heart infection that was never properly diagnosed. Not an uncommon way for an immigrant to die in working-class Queens, where exhaustion and stress could turn minor ailments into life-threatening conditions. The overburdened docs at Elmhurst General just made a snap diagnosis, wrote out a death certificate, and moved on to the next crisis. This had happened about five years previously; Maggie remembered her dad fondly but not very clearly.

After struggling for a while to keep the business afloat, her mom had to sell but couldn't fully pay off her loan. So the family had debt, utility bills, and rent to deal with, not to mention the expenses associated with raising a kid. Meanwhile Chen basically gave up and sank into what sounded like a depression. He demanded cash for food and beer and contributed nothing. Her mother issued ultimatums; Chen ignored her, sometimes contemptuously.

The murky shit with her mom was pretty much as Esther had described it. She was never home in the evenings and was blind to the creepy situation with Chen, maybe willfully. She was forced to earn cash by doing something shady, something she would never talk about. Maggie had suspicions but didn't want to think too hard about what it might be; she had a notion that Chen knew all about it and was using that knowledge to threaten and humiliate his sister-in-law.

"Can't she get something semi-legit, with regular daytime hours? Plenty of people around here are working without papers."

"She says we can't make the loan payments on minimum wage. Plus, she has no self-confidence. After my dad died, she tried to move on to something new. Like, she got an online certificate in library science and sent out a bunch of applications. But no one wrote back and she was crushed. Now she's always down on herself. It's like she thinks she doesn't deserve any better. And Chen undermines her; tells her she's no good."

By now, every moment Maggie spent at home with Chen hanging around was torture. He lurked, followed her from room to room, pretending to be interested in her schoolwork just so he could intrude on her personal space. Recently he'd begun to interrogate her about her schedule and her friends; he wanted her to account for everything she did outside of the house. Confronting her on the street Saturday night was just the latest escalation.

"Esther told me some of this stuff," I admitted. "Please don't be mad at her. She didn't want to betray your trust, but she had to tell somebody to keep from freaking out entirely. She swore me to secrecy, so obviously I'll keep it on the DL. I hope it's all right with you. I'm afraid she's going to hate me for approaching you about it."

"It's okay, Moses. I'm crazy embarrassed about it but I suppose it had to come out sooner or later. It's almost a relief. And if she had to tell somebody, I'm glad it was you. You're the nicest guy I know; you've been a real friend since Middle School."

"Okay, this is really awkward, but I have to ask. Do you feel like he's going to try to, well, try something physical any time soon?"

"Esther is sure that he will, sooner or later. She says that's the pattern. I don't know. I don't feel like I'm under any kind of immediate threat, if that's what you mean. And I don't want the authorities getting in our business if we can possibly avoid it."

Her face fell; she was again on the verge of tears. "This is *so* messed up. I just hate it."

Maggie was so obviously in need of comfort that I reached across the table and touched her hand without thinking about it. Mistake. She tensed and pulled back. I won't lie; that hurt.

"Mose, please don't take offense, but what I need right now is a friend, not a boyfriend. Besides, Esther would kill me."

"Meaning?"

"I'm not supposed to tell you this, but Esther is, well, kind of interested in you."

What the hell? It didn't seem possible. Esther was formidable, gorgeous, amply skilled; I thought of myself as a klutzy, neurotic jumble of trivial obsessions with little more than a kickass vocabulary to recommend me.

"I can't believe it. I mean, she's totally out of my league."

"Oh, really?" Maggie raised an eyebrow. "And I'm not?"

I struggled to extricate my big fat foot from my big fat mouth.

"That's not what I meant. You're amazing in every way; I've always thought so. It's just that I've never doubted that you actually *like* me; half the time I feel like Esther thinks I'm a complete asshat."

"Far from it, Mose. She thinks you're cute and funny, and the fact that you actually seem to respect women sets you apart from most of the guys. She likes you a lot, but she won't let on because she's afraid of rejection. That's why she talks to you that way. It's like the flipside of P.D. He needs to act super-cool all the time because he's so vulnerable. He couldn't stand to be ridiculed or hurt."

Mind blown. Again I felt like a self-absorbed navel-gazer; evidently I couldn't even read my closest friends.

"Don't tell her I told you, Mose. If you want to do anything about it, it's all on you."

The idea of Esther being scared of anything, especially mild-mannered Moses Middleton, was stupefying. In the immortal words of The Dude, new shit had come to light. I was intrigued af, and a little confused to be honest, but I needed to put all this aside for consideration at a later time. The clock was running; I still had some boxes to tick.

Returning to the matter at hand, I raised the issue of finding her mom a gig. Maggie filled me in on her résumé. She had the equivalent of a master's degree in microbiology, knew her way around programming, and had done plenty of research back in China. If she could have used her student visa to actually study, she'd probably be working in a lab at some American university by now. Instead, she had a massive hole in her job history and no way to get back on track in academics.

I wondered, though, if her background might be enough for an entry-level research position at some private biomed firm, of which there were a couple gadzillion in New York City. It would be a lowly joint for someone with her qualifications, but it had to be better than doing something she was ashamed of. Maybe my dad could help? Maggie gave me the okay to run it past him in an exploratory way; he didn't need to know the grimy details, just that she was looking to patch up her C.V. with something, anything, in her field.

I paid the check and dropped Maggie off at her place, one of those gruesome cookie-cutter Fedders buildings in Corona. Asked her to text me wit da quickness if she ever felt something really unpleasant was about to go down. She agreed. She even gave me a quick goodbye hug; evidently some forms of physical contact were okay inside the Friend Zone so long as she was the initiator. I could respect that, especially considering the non-stop skeeviness she was forced to deal with at home.

Nothing was resolved, but at least I'd taken another step along the critical path. That would have to be good enough for one day. Back in my room, I suddenly realized I was monumentally shagged out. It had been a week of ceaseless agita with a series of tasks that were, well, Herculean. And there was more to come.

Now I knew how the Hercmeister felt when he'd finished ten labors and that vindictive little turd Eurystheus ordered him to do two more. If you've watched any of the Italian screen epics, you'd figure that Hercules spent all his time uncorking huge bottles of whoopass on a variety of villains and (badly animated) monsters. The part the movies don't cover is 12 long years of busting his ass for The Man. Story was, the goddess Hera hated my dude because he was the illegitimate, half-mortal son of her husband, Zeus. For payback, she drove him crazy and made him kill his own sons. Once he regained his sanity, Herc, devastated, visited the oracle at Delphi (that's my mom's usual cosplay character) and was told he needed to do shitwork for some jumped-up tyrant named Eurystheus, who had stolen his throne. Eurystheus assigned him ten humiliating, seemingly impossible jobs. The more disgusting, the better — like cleaning mountains of cow shit from the stables of mad King Augeus. Once all ten labors were in the bag, the boss decided he'd bent the rules and gave him extra homework. Ten labors became 12. Upshot is, Hercules wasn't your typical ass-kicking hero guy; he had to *work* for it. I settled on my bed for what I thought would be a brief nap; experienced a major adrenal crash.

Next thing I knew it was early evening and I was being summoned to the kitchen for salad prep. This was my dad's night to cook, and as always he was staging an elaborate production, playing the master chef as he finessed his locally famous slide-off-the-bone oven barbecued ribs. It was too cold for the backyard grill, but he was nevertheless going Full Dad in his grill gear, complete with joke toque and adorkable apron — plus, to my horror, Crocs. He and Mom were getting playfully affectionate (*cringe*) while he worked the tongs and spatula; she thought he was sexy when he was in geek mode. The ribs were sick delicious and my Greek salad was a hit; for dessert, Julian and Allegra had collaborated on a *chajá*, a sponge cake layered with whipped cream and dulce de leche. Ritwik regaled us with crazy shaggy-dog stories from his childhood in India and had the whole table in stitches. I ate myself into a state of near-oblivion and blissed out on the sugar rush, though I had a fleeting sense of worry that I might be starting a belly if I didn't watch out. Weird: This had never been a problem for me — my supercharged metabolism was the envy of my peers — but I guess I was thinking about Esther's sculpted athleticism and wondering if I could possibly measure up. And then I remembered Zamir's tee: "Why turn down? I am fabulous!" Just one little hint from Maggie and my worldview had undergone a seismic shift. That's adolescence for yiz.

After cleanup I cornered my dad and outlined the situation with Maggie's mom. Strictly need-to-know; I omitted the Chen situation and the dubious nighttime gig. The way I framed it, she was just eager to get back into the job market after a long lapse and wouldn't be picky about a low-level job so long as it was more or less in her field.

"Tell Maggie she should get me a C.V. Doesn't have to be elaborate, and she can be honest about the gap for child-raising. I'll bring it up with my boss; she's the furthest thing from a corporate drone. She likes to help people with issues; we might be able to work something out."

Dad worked at this huge nonprofit that preserved and distributed biological materials, mostly microorganisms and cell lines for medical research. When he left Cold Spring Harbor, he'd been heavily recruited by Big Pharma firms. But after hearing their pitches he concluded that most of them were just manufacturing poisons for profit. So he turned down the big bucks and found job he liked, one that he could live with from an ethical point of view. His firm hired a lot of new grads, immigrants, and career changers; the company culture was pretty woke. I mentioned the green card issue.

"Might not be a problem. As it happens, my boss is a passionate supporter of immigration reform. It goes back to Trump. She hates ICE and she's been advocating for the DREAM Act for years. Her position on hiring immigrants is strictly 'don't ask, don't tell.' If she likes an applicant, they just need to produce a half-way plausible I-9 Form. That's going to be good enough for her. One more thing: That certificate in library science could be a plus. We're kind of like a library, only with microbes instead of books."

He could see the excitement on my face and added a caution. "No promises, Mose. But it's absolutely worth a try."

Later I texted the gist to Maggie; she said she'd try to broach the issue. It would be delicate, she was sure, but I urged her — gently but firmly, like my mom always says — to go for it. Went to bed feeling like I'd accomplished a lot; lulled myself to sleep with thoughts of chess, dreamily imagining positions, trying to be one with the board like some Bodhisattva Botvinnik. Four more days till The Return of the Mad Commie Chess Monster.

11. SEEING RED

"We will begin with an exercise, one that was highly effective in sharpening the skills of young players in the Pioneer Palace. In English it is simply called 'Rotation.' Moses, kindly set up three boards and arrange chairs around the table."

I did so. It was Thursday night and we were diving right in. I was psyched. For once the week had sped by without any unpleasant incidents. My Volonté presentation went over well — especially the gunfight, needless to say — and a couple of kids even asked for YouTube links afterwards. We all thought of movies as a relatively painless way to learn Italian, and I felt good about spreading the Volonté gospel. All week I'd kept my guard up for the inevitable confrontation with Marco and Steve, but no drama had transpired. Yet. I was chill and ready for chess.

"Let us pair off at the boards," Viktor said. "I will take one of the places so that we will have an even number."

We grabbed seats, more or less randomly, and I found myself across from Viktor. Always an intimidating place to be.

"Each of us will play three moves. Then we will rotate one seat counterclockwise and play three more moves. We will repeat this process so long as the games continue. If a game has concluded, simply wait — you may, of course analyze the final position — and then rotate when the remaining active players have completed their moves."

As he spoke, Viktor studied each of us with his keen, borderline scary blue eyes. "As you studied the Botvinnik chapter in your Bible, you will have noticed his remarkable ability to grasp positions, to read potentials and fields of force across all 64 squares. This exercise will train your mind by forcing you to do the same. Too much of your thinking is linear: 'I will do this, then she will do that.' The aim here is to think dialectically. Survey the whole board, comprehend the dynamics of the opposing forces, divine the manner in which those forces are likely to clash and reconcile. You will have one minute for each move."

A sweeping gesture, like a bullfighter brandishing his cape. "Gentlemen and gentlewomen, have at it."

Viktor opened with d4, and I thought I'd try to impress him with the Nimzo-Indian, advancing my king's knight. Viktor responded with c4, as you'd expect, seizing control of the center. Things proceeded by the book; I was looking to trade off my dark-squared bishop in order to damage his pawn structure and hopefully get a lead in development. Just as things were starting to get interesting, it was time to play musical chairs.

I found myself sitting across from P.D., playing white and looking at a classic Ruy Lopez. I took a breath and tried hard to grok the overall dynamics, as Viktor advised. All I could really see at this stage of the game was that I should try to mess up black's pawn structure. So I took the classic route and traded bishop for knight, ceding P.D. the bishop pair in the hope of exploiting his now doubled pawn. I held my own, I thought, through a couple more moves.

Third rotation. I sat down across from Zamir, and *bang!* I found myself right in the thick of a complex opening. It was like one of those combat video games. I'd parachuted into the middle of a chaotic firefight and had seconds to survey the LZ and make sense of the situation. For a moment I felt panicky; my eyes darted around the board looking for threats. This was *not* working. Time for some Zen. Got hold of myself, took a deep breath, sat back and tried to absorb the whole position. Good. Touched the Pushkin medal. Better. Now I was beginning to understand what Viktor wanted to teach us. The board, I sensed, was in a state of equilibrium. A balance of forces existed; the initiative was mine. I developed a knight, attacking one of Zamir's pawns. He defended, simultaneously launching a counterattack. Suddenly it was time for the next board; it was up to P.D. to cope with whatever nefarious scheme Zamir was unleashing.

The rotations continued. Sometimes I thought I was experiencing the magic of The Zone, sensing the fundamentals of a position at a glance; mostly I had to find a move by mental brute force. Once I screwed up badly, missing a piece *en prise*. Eventually, seated in front of the final position of a finished game, I had a moment to breathe. I looked around the table. Not unexpectedly, P.D. and Zamir appeared entirely chill: they were already comfortable with this kind of thinking. Esther was glaring at the board with knitted brows; Maggie, I noticed with interest, looked rapt. She was *getting* it.

After the exercise wrapped, Viktor polled us for our reactions. Zamir, it seemed, had had the time of his life; P.D. flashed a thumbs-up; Esther grudgingly conceded that she'd learned something. Maggie, somewhat to my surprise, was absolutely geeked.

"It was like *Star Wars*!" she exclaimed. "I just surrendered to The Force and I saw what to do."

Viktor grinned. "It is indeed a force, but it is in no wise supernatural, and it does not come from the outside. Every human mind has the capacity to synthesize information, to perceive the patterns that underlie the surface of reality. To some of us it comes naturally; to others, it becomes possible through training and repetition. Within each of you, one might say, there is a little Botvinnik wildly signaling to get out."

"I now propose to pluck some low-hanging fruit. What I say will be obvious to some of you, but it is a type of basic strategic analysis that will increase your chances if borne in mind and implemented faithfully. It is, I confess, a vulgar emulation of what Botvinnik was able to do with his computer programs."

He gestured toward my laptop. "In the local library I was able to access considerable information using the internet. Among other things, I reviewed recent tournaments of your Chess in the Schools program. Several things became clear. First, there are virtually no draws at this level of play. At the grandmaster level, the first-move advantage is so powerful that one almost invariably seeks to draw when playing black. Scholastic chess is a different beast entirely. The better players gain material advantages quickly and exploit them. It is possible to mount a credible defense by complicating the position, but in 30-minute games there is rarely enough time on the clock to force a draw in this manner."

"In Soviet team play, we were taught that securing the half-point on black was nearly as good as a win. Karpov, for example, was a master of forcing the draw and typically played Caro-Kann or Petrov's Defense because these openings tend to undermine white's initiative and blunt his aggression."

Viktor illustrated his points by arranging pieces on the board as he spoke, whipping out the main lines of Caro-Kann and Petrov's at lightning speed.

"These are sensible, historically proven openings for black. Yet at your level, it is pointless to play them because the draw is so rarely attainable. I conclude that aggression with the black pieces is far more likely to be rewarded than sound defensive play."

"Second, in scholastic tournaments I am astonished by how frequently white plays for the scholar's mate – that is, e4; e5; Qh5. This is, of course, a trap for beginners only." (I cringed internally, remembering my recent pooch-screw.) "But a shocking number of players are so eager for the quick, crushing checkmate that it is their preferred opening for white. If you have not already done so, spare a few minutes to learn how to counter this foolhardy aggression. You may easily disrupt white's plan this with g6; proceed to harass white's exposed queen; develop your queen's bishop; et cetera. The initiative will be yours and a path to victory should open presently."

"Third, I would advise you never to resign under any circumstances. This is difficult, I know, partly because resignation strikes us as the polite thing to do in an apparently hopeless position, and partly because it is so painful to play out a lost game to the bitter end. Yet I observed a remarkable number of games that were won on time or drawn by stalemate because the player with the material advantage had not committed basic endgame tactics to heart. Stubbornly playing on and hoping for the blunder appears to be surprisingly effective at the scholastic level. Conversely, you yourselves must know your endgame through and through. For example, each of you must be able to checkmate with king and rook with speed and absolute confidence."

"With due respect, Mr. Fleischmann, this is all baby stuff," P.D. said.

"You are not wrong. But comprehensive mastery of the baby stuff will free your mind to grapple with more interesting problems. Michelangelo would have made hundreds of sketches before attempting a fresco or attacking a block of marble."

Viktor asked me to pull up the list of tournament entrants on my laptop.

"I note that the schools participating in this tournament are very much like yours. You will not be facing the exclusive private institutions favored by the city's ruling class; nor will you encounter the notoriously powerful teams from Harlem and Brooklyn. You have every chance to perform respectably; in fact, I anticipate that you will finish among the top three."

Esther looked dubious. "We've never finished anywhere near the top three in any tournament we've entered. Why should this one be any different?"

"Because, my dear, you are already becoming a team rather than a random collection of individuals. You will draw strength from one another, and you will play with discipline and enthusiasm because you will not wish to disappoint your comrades."

Esther nodded and I caught myself darting a sidewise glance at her, registering like never before how hot she was. Instantly her eyes flicked over in my direction; I looked away automatically but too late. I could feel the blood rushing to my face. I reminded myself, for the millionth time, that you can never get away with ogling a girl surreptitiously. They always know; it's like a sixth sense. I try really hard not to be a creep but at my age it's all but impossible to stop yourself checking girls out. It's instinctual, I guess. I swallowed my embarrassment as Viktor continued his spiel.

"There is more. I am about to impose upon you a collective strategy. Here is what I will require: For the first three rounds, each of you will play the Danish Gambit on white and the Scandinavian Defense on black. These openings, as you will have seen, are confrontational. The immediate sacrifice of a center pawn, or two, is disruptive, likely to unsettle your opponent's state of mind. You will seize the initiative and press your psychological advantage with continued aggression. These openings are not played at the grandmaster level, because their flaws have long since been exposed by analysis. But I am convinced that you will find them highly effective in scholastic play."

"What if I'm on black and white plays something other than e4?" I asked.

"Then the Scandinavian is out."

"In this case you must play an appropriate defense with which you are comfortable. This is unlikely to happen, by the way. The scholastic games I reviewed suggested that white plays e4 approximately 90 percent of the time. When he doesn't, it is typically the Queen's Gambit, so I would advise you to study this opening as well."

P.D. looked doubtful. "Suppose we play these openings and get rekt anyway?"

"You will return to your table, analyze with a teammate, and learn from your mistakes. Win or lose, find a partner and play though your games. Then press onward. You must adhere to your overall strategy, even in the face of tactical setbacks."

"This kinda reminds me of baseball," I ventured. "You can hit a perfect line drive like you practiced a million times, but you're unlucky and it happens to fly right into the fielder's glove. They call it 'good process, bad outcome.' You don't throw away your whole approach just because of one lousy result. If you stick with the good process, over time you get where you need to be."

"I know nothing of baseball, Moses, but this has the ring of truth. Consistency is critical."

Zamir spoke up. "Mr. Fleischmann, you said we should play these openings for the first three rounds. What about the fourth?"

"It is possible that some of you may win three games and find yourself paired with very strong players in the final round. You may well encounter an opponent who will not be overawed by aggression as such. In this case I would wish to grant you the option of opening as you think best."

"Another factor will likely arise. After three rounds, I would venture to guess the enemy will have noticed by that you are playing the same openings in coordination. The abler players and the well-coached teams will attempt a quick study of the Danish and the Scandinavian. They will come to the board anticipating one thing; you will perhaps do something entirely different. Once again, your opponent will be disoriented. I am reminded of so-called 'Match of the Century,' in which your brash young genius thwarted us by opening with c4, the English opening. Fischer *always* played e4 on white; all our preparation hinged on that fact; consequently, we were ambushed when he pushed that bishop's pawn. You have a similar opportunity to lay a strategic trap."

"You really think those guys will figure out what we're doing, let alone care what we're doing?" P.D. asked skeptically. "We're nobodies."

"No longer. Q722 is about to emerge from the shadows. I am quite confident that you will create a stir, a flurry of interest. You will be discussed nervously between rounds. That, too, will work to your advantage. Anyone paired with a Q722 player will be wary. Possibly intimidated." A sinister chuckle, like a movie villain. "This, I assure you, will be a pleasant experience."

"There is one more thing I will ask of you. Dress as a team; wear the school colors perhaps. This will alert your opponents that they will be facing a united force, one that must be reckoned with."

Esther rolled her eyes. "As if we're not geeky enough already."

"We will be proudly geeky," said Zamir, grinning. "Together."

Surprising myself, I was up for this. Dressing up like some dorky robotics team would be a statement. After all, one of the things I admired most about P.D. was his complete contempt for what the socs thought of him. I wanted to emulate him; it was my chance to give the world a finger.

"The school has polo shirts with our crest, such as it is, but they're mad expensive," Maggie pointed out. "Something like fifty bucks apiece."

"I think I may have a solution to that problem," I said. "Leave it to me."

P.D. shot me an ironic glance. "Mose, you seem to have forgotten the Three Rules of Survival: Never order fish on a Monday. Never check your dad's browser history. Never volunteer."

"For my beloved teammates I'm ready to break any and all rules, comrade. Suitable attire will be provided; count on it."

As we broke for the evening, Maggie asked Viktor whether he would come with us to the tournament. He declined. He wanted us to win for ourselves and each other, he explained; his presence would be a distraction. I was disappointed, as was Maggie, but I got his point. I'd seen the teams that always played with their coaches riding herd. The kids seemed cowed — in some cases all but terrorized — by overbearing authority figures who sucked the air out of the room. Viktor wasn't like that, of course, but even so I sensed that we would be empowered if compelled to lean on our own resources. All for one and one for all; you know the drill.

Next project: I had to get my hands on some matching custom T-shirts for the team. I checked online and discovered that I'd need to raise at least fiddy bucks to make the nut. Suddenly I saw the wisdom of P.D.'s warning about volunteering. That was a lot of ching-ching under the best of circumstances, and this week I was hurting for pocket change. Hated to do it, but I busted open the virtual piggy bank, selling most of the coin I'd accumulated during a brief phase of crypto enthusiasm. Dashed off to the print shop; put in a rush order for five shirts. Made sure they weren't using that brand that employs Haitian sweatshop labor and terrorizes the unions; no way Esther would wear one of those. Chose red, which happened to be our school color but seemed appropriate for other reasons, haha.

So that was a wrap. Just needed to negotiate one more school day and we'd be good to go.

* * *

As it happened, making it through Friday was a bigger challenge than I'd expected. Halfway through the morning I whipped out to the street for a quick vape and, by sheer chance, caught the Evil Twins pushing Zamir around by the dumpsters. Steve had Zamir's arms pinned while Marco was cuffing him around the face. A mouse had already appeared under one of his eyes; it felt like a fullscale beatdown was in the offing.

This time I didn't stop to think. Lost it like Romo; I was too goddam mad to be scared. I stepped in and grabbed Marco by the shoulder.

"You human ... paraquat!" I barked, falling back on a Lebowski line in my sputtering fury. "What the hell is the *point* of you, anyway?"

Marco looked taken aback. I don't think he'd ever seen me raging; it can't have been a pretty sight. I probably should have kept my mouth shut, but I was torqued outta control.

"Here's the answer, Marco: There's *no* point. You're just a turd with earlobes. You're not good for anything. You have zero skills. The girls all think you're a skeeve. You don't have any friends except for Lurch over here. You're a completely worthless twonk and you waste the air you breathe."

"Yeah? Well, up yours, Middleton," he retorted. Dazzling repartee FTW. He squared up and I took a step toward him, too angry for once to worry about preserving my health and boyish good looks. I raised my fists.

"Bring it on, you no-neck moron."

It was over in two seconds. He nailed me with a brutal overhand right and I was down like Duane Bobick. Everything went quiet for a couple of beats as I cleared my head, checked various parts of my body to see if anything was broken, and slowly struggled to my feet.

"Had enough, you wonky little puss?" Marco sneered.

Here was the part where I was supposed to cry uncle and slink away, humiliated. But I was still too pissed off to do the sensible thing. Seeing red for sure.

"The real question is, have *you* had enough?" I stepped in and threw a wild roundhouse punch — I don't know the first thing about fighting, so I was just improvising thoughtlessly — and, by pure luck, I connected solidly with Marco's cheekbone.

In the movies, the bully invariably turns coward and runs away at the slightest sign of resistance from his victim. That's not how it works in real life. Marco was clearly shaken up but he didn't go down or back off. Instead he staggered forward, grabbed me around the neck, and administered a headbutt to my chin. The blow landed awkwardly but hurt like a muffa. He drew back, rubbing his cheek. We were both gasping, but I managed to spit out a reckless little speech, piped directly to my mouth from my overheated lizard brain.

"Listen to me, you pathetic excuse for a gangsta. From now on, any time you mess with me, or any of my friends, there *will* be consequences. I know you'll probably always hurt me more than I can hurt you, but I don't really give a shit. I will take the punishment, every time, if it means you don't get to run around the school victimizing people like some kind of cheap Nazi action figure."

"Don't make me laugh, dicktard. I'm gonna keep coming at you whenever I feel like it."

Instead of escalating, though, he wheeled and booked off, with Steve trailing behind. He flipped a parting finger. A surprisingly feeble response, in my judgment. Far from a victory for Mad Moses, but maybe I'd earned a little respect.

Pulled out the phone and surveyed my face in selfie mode. Not bad; no visible damage that I would need to explain to my parents. I was hurting in various places, yet still standing and fundamentally intact. Same for Zamir, though a manly shiner looked inevitable. His T-shirt was stretched out of shape and torn, though, which was a damn shame — it was the best shirt yet, emblazoned with the immortal slogan: "Blame it on youthness."

So were pretty okay for the moment. I realized, however, that we were playing on a whole new level; a titanic boss battle couldn't be far off. Like a fool, I'd thrown fists and shot off my mouth. I was committed now, not just on my own behalf but for my friends as well. And I couldn't back down: If I wimped out, I'd be Marco's bitch forever.

Yet I'd done the right thing, I knew deep down in my kishkas, and as a result I was feeling righteous and weirdly strong. I'd lost my head because it wasn't just *my* head anymore. I'd acted for all of us. It was a little uncanny, to be honest — I felt like the combined spirit of all my teammates was flowing through me, giving me strength, pushing me forward. I'd surrendered to the power of the collective. Another dose of Commie Zen, as instilled by Roshi Fleischmann.

Zamir, looking stricken, asked if I needed to go to the school nurse. Told him no; warned him that any official interest in the fight could result in suspensions. We somehow had to handle it on our own. Besides, narking was strictly prohibited in the Middleton Code of Personal Conduct. In New York City, I advised him, snitches get stitches. It was no different in Albania, he assured me. That was why he'd stood up and declined to whine about previous episodes of harassment.

"I don't need to tell you that this is far from over, dawg. I don't know where it's going. I'm reluctant to call on P.D. as our enforcer; he's bound to hurt somebody and he'll end up expelled, or worse. I'm not sure there's a happy ending here."

Zamir looked thoughtful. "We must reflect and plan, as we would in a chess game. Or a guerilla war. My ancestors fought in the hills against superior enemies for centuries. Sometimes direct confrontation — am I saying this right? — is not the best tactic. I am thinking about something I could do that might divide the enemy forces."

"Pray tell."

Zamir shook his head inscrutably. "If it works, you will know."

We were running late so we hustled inside. It was strange to be back in the classroom, sharpening pencils and solving algebra problems, after the morning's melodrama. I guess even Hercules had mundane tasks to accomplish when he wasn't strangling monstrous beasts with his bare hands.

I was able to check in with Maggie, Esther, and P.D. during the course of a long afternoon. Everyone felt ready to execute Viktor's strategy on the morrow. Maggie in particular was out for blood; she got closer to talking trash than I'd imagined possible. The Fleischmann Effect was in the house. Queens scholastic chess was about to get rocked.

12. ALL FOR ONE AND ONE FOR ALL

Saturday dawned at last. Oddly, my nervous stomach wasn't acting up that morning; I was psyched for the tournament but not, it seemed, psyched out. Blasted through the cleansing rituals and genuflected before Campy's shrine, praying for juju. Checked my look in the mirror: passable. I was as ready as I was going to be.

Fortified by a double-shot cappuccino, I coasted over to Zamir's place so I could lead him to Sunnyside, a tree-lined neighborhood of single-family homes that was undergoing a milder version of the gentrification plague that had infected Jackson Heights. Q150 was surprisingly big for a K-6; it turned out to be one of those ponderous (*eat my vocab, losers!*) pre-war, foursquare brick joints that you'll find all over Queens. It had one real distinction: A big, eye-catching social realist mural of schoolkids learning and doing. It was created in 1940 with U.S. government funds, I later learned, but it wouldn't have been wildly out of place in one of Viktor's Pioneer Palaces.

I knew about this stuff because of my lefty grandparents, who were fanatics about New York City public art. A couple of times they'd dragooned me into grueling, seemingly endless walking tours of Manhattan. (Bataan Death Marches, my mom called them; she'd been forced into similar excursions as a kid.) They never tired of pointing out the radical themes behind statues and murals left over from the Depression — like, say, the trippy stained-glass windows in Bayard Rustin High School on West 18th Street. Their lectures had been a drag, but some of it sank in, so I was always on the lookout for specimens and reported back to them whenever I found a good one. It was another example of the secret history, revealing traces of a socialist New Yitty that remained invisible to most. The way Grandpa and Grandma explained it, it wasn't like the city fathers had all gone wild-eyed Red during the 1930s; actually, socialist values were so widely shared at the time that the rich dudes figured public art needed to reflect how the people were thinking — or else maybe the people would start thinking about kicking some rich dude butt.

On closer examination, though, the mural was a major disappointment. Unlike a lot of the radical art from the era, all the kids depicted were white. Pretty lame, especially for a school that was now mostly Asian and Hispanic. One girl was shown in the foreground making a sculpture, but otherwise the young women were all learning household tasks — what they used to call "home ec" — while only the boys got to wield mighty tools and build cool stuff. My grandparents would've written this one off as unenlightened at best.

Still, something really hit me about the painting: its confidence, its unqualified optimism. Even on the brink of a world war, these students were building a better future together. My classmates aren't like this. We don't really believe in anything; we figure it's all happy-face bullshit that's supposed to keep us obedient. Copium for the masses. We're not sure we even *have* a future. Instead we have stuff. Mostly electronic stuff that keeps us isolated, focused on our little screens. The kids I knew who were joiners, who got active in volunteer mills with slogans like "Be the Change" or "Shaping a Better World," were mostly faking it; they were stacking résumé bullets to accelerate their careers. A pretense of collective effort as cover for personal ambition. Thinking about the depressing world I lived in, I got a sense of what Viktor was missing, why he'd lost his marbles and hit the streets when everything he believed in got blown away. Would I trade all my stuff for a world like the one he grew up in? Well, please don't put a gun to my head: I sure do like my stuff — what little I have, that is.

Anyhow, the interior of 150 was kind of imposing, roomy and built to last. It even had decent heating, unlike the clanky, steam-spitting radiators in 722. A suitable site for combat. We got there early so we could annex a good table in the lunchroom. If we were going to carry out Viktor's command to analyze our games between rounds, we'd need plenty of space to spread our boards and stretch out. As Zamir and I skittled, the girls arrived in full BFF mode, with Esther's arm draped protectively over Maggie's shoulder. Man, they were beautiful in every sense of the word; I could feel a bigtime idiot grin spreading across my face as I waved them over.

"Really, Mose, you look like you just huffed a gigantic snort of E," Esther said.

"You know I would never defile my perfect body with foreign substances, bar the occasional hit of bubblegum e-juice."

"Pictures of perfection make me sick and wicked, dear boy," she Austened.

There was no way I could top that, so I was a kinda relieved when P.D., running on Daylate Savings Time as usual, swooped in. He was throwing styles like Miles, having accessorized his beat-up army jacket with a red silk scarf. On me it probably would've looked ridiculous; on him — ice cold and darkly handsome — it was a fashion plate. He was bright-eyed despite the early hour. For once he didn't even smell like weed.

"Me little droogies," he greeted us. "Are we ready for redrum?"

Whoa, a double-barrelled Kubrick reference. Impressive. I countered with some HercSpeak.

"They will cower before us, brave Hylas. *Nessuno mi unfungulo.*"

"Given my own preferences, homes, I can't endorse that sentiment. But if you mean we're going to strafe the playing fields like a squadron of F-16s, I'm your man."

Maggie giggled. "Say the hank of hair thing, Moses."

She was requesting one of my overworn fallback phrases, one that for some reason she found endlessly amusing.

"With pleasure." I cleared my throat and declaimed: "By the time we're done with these guys, there'll be nothing left but a hank of hair, some teeth, and a small dark oily stain."

With that I reached for my shopping bag, broke out the T-shirts I'd commissioned, and passed them around, noting expressions ranging from amusement to shock as my teammates comprehended the sheer horror of what I'd done. On the front: "Q722: GRANDMASTER FLEISCH AND THE FURIOUS FIVE." On the back: "WE ARE BECOMING WINNER." Everything rendered in gloriously nerdy Comic Sans, gold on red like our school colors — not to mention the Soviet flag. This was going to be a statement for sure.

"Compliments of the Middleton Foundation, comrades. Wear them in good health."

"You have *got* to be kidding," Esther said. "Team solidarity is one thing, but this is just inviting ridicule."

Zamir looked crestfallen; he obviously dug the shirts and could tell that I'd been inspired by his bangin' Balkan gear.

"No point in half-measures when you're clowning out," I replied in defense. "I'd rather be ridiculed for truly epic geekiness than sneered at for a mildly cornball gesture. These shirts carry a message for our opponents. And that message is: Screw you."

"*Hell* yeah," exclaimed P.D., donning his shirt while flashing an ironic leer. "May the dorks be with you."

I was grateful. If the coolest dude at 722 was on board with the prank, the rest of us dweebs could have no grounds for complaint. Zamir was beaming again.

"I'm going to go out on a limb right now and make a prediction," I said. "If we end up winning this thing, you're going to see other schools sporting copycat shirts at the next tournament. They'll be thinking it's some kind of magic charm."

Esther looked dubious but sighed, slipped into her tee, and settled the matter with some high-grade Austening.

"For what do we live, but to make sport for our neighbors, and laugh at them in our turn?"

I could get behind that. She favored me with a raised eyebrow and just the hint of a smile. I won't pretend it didn't make my little heart go pitter-pat. Quietly I asked her whether Maggie had had any more issues with creepy Uncle Chen. Nothing major, she said. In fact, Maggie thought he was glad to see her go today; probably wanted to be alone with Stripchat. *Yech.*

Kids from other schools began to arrive in force. I noticed a couple of curious stares attracted by our kitschy excuses for uniforms, but no overt expressions of derision. Yet. This tournament was just for Queens publics, so no Stuyvesant, no Hunter High, no Adam Clayton Powell, Jr. — and, of course, no Galton Prep. There were a couple of strong teams, though, notably some disciplined youngsters from Hillcrest in Jamaica and a squad from Queens High School for the Sciences. Some big teams, too, though only the top four scores from each school would count toward the team championship. It was easy to see that these were kids like us. As Viktor had suggested, we wouldn't be facing down the class enemy today; this was instead a chance to test our prowess and sharpen our skills before taking on the superboss. We had a legit chance of doing well against these guys, I felt sure, and if we showed up winners today it would do wonders for our morale.

A sudden noisy rush for the scorer's table; pairings had been posted. Zamir wriggled his way to the front and noted down our boards and colors. He came back smiling, hyped for action as he shared the info and wished us luck.

I drew black against a South Asian kid from Newtown High in Elmhurst. I eyed him warily as we settled over the board. This dude was, like, *mature.* Well over six feet with a shaggy full beard. Had to be a senior. I took a deep breath, summoned my inner Botvinnik, and simply refused to be intimidated.

So when he opened, as expected, with the king's pawn, I jumped right in with d5, putting my queen's pawn on the chopping block and going right on the attack. Scandy in the house. Right away the magic happened. He froze. Stared at the board, head in hands, as five minutes ticked off the clock. I'd freaked him out; clearly it was his first encounter with the Scandinavian. He suspected a trap, I figured, and was scared to grab my pawn even though it was the most sensible response. Eventually he sighed, looking like a beaten man already, and captured. Instantly I snatched his king's pawn with my queen, slapping the clock with a blitz master's flourish. This was mad aggression on my part, and I wanted to heighten the psychological pressure with brisk, assertive play.

Another long pause. He'd be feeling time pressure pretty soon if he continued like this. Finally, still sighing and sucking his teeth, he made a decent move, deploying a knight to attack my queen, doubtless hoping I'd been reckless with my most valuable piece and that he could now chase her around the board. Since I knew the opening inside and out, I was once again able to respond almost instantaneously, snapping my queen down on the a5 square and punching the clock. This kind of macho showmanship was something I absolutely hated when an opponent did it to me. But that was just the point: I wanted him to believe that I knew exactly what I was doing and was anticipating his every move.

After another agonizing pause, he essayed his own little gambit, threatening my queen with b4. *Bang!* I erased his pawn and then settled back in my chair theatrically. I wanted to get inside his head, convince him that I already had the game in hand. It worked. Within a couple of moves he had blundered away a piece, and the rest was a foregone conclusion. He resigned, looking so disconsolate that I almost felt sorry for him. I offered my hand and thanked him, sincerely, for the game, dropping the cocky façade.

Tear off the shrink wrap and crack the box: The brand new edition of Moses Middleton had arrived. I'd always played carefully, conservatively, relying on sound opening strategy to build and exploit small advantages. Now I was sallying forth like a half-mad street spieler. Viktor's tournament strategy had unleashed my inner Magnus Carlsen and I liked the way it made me feel. I would need to watch this, I thought: I didn't want to evolve into some egotistical dickbrain like Marco. I hoped to improve myself, sure, but I wanted to stay nice. Whatever it was that Esther liked about me was not something I wanted to mess with. It occurred to me that the dumbest cliché about women is the idea that they're into the arrogant, self-important dudes who treat them contemptuously. That convenient myth had probably been invented by jerkoffs like Marco as a way of rationalizing their sociopathic behavior.

I popped outside for a hasty vape and found P.D. and Zamir in a huddle, looking for all the world like best buds as they compared notes on their games. Like me, they'd implemented Viktor's strategy and were rewarded with quick, decisive wins. Zamir's opponent, an overconfident kid with a fairly impressive Elo, had ventured a snarky remark about the T-shirt. In response, Zamir coolly put his lights out. I checked his scoresheet. His first tournament game amply confirmed what Viktor saw in him; he was a natural with mad potential.

We returned to our table together and ran some analysis. Our games were similar: In each case the opponents seemed baffled by our non-standard openings and blundered early. So far, so good. Shortly the girls showed up, throwing swagger: They'd both won. Holy shit, we were 5-0. I could hardly believe it.

We played through their games, elated. Esther had run into some trouble in the middle game, seemingly as a result of trying too hard to win back the sacrificed pawn, but in the end her aggressive development yielded opportunities. Maggie had *killed.* She'd harried her opponent with both bishops, creating cover for a crushing attack right up the center with rook and queen. It was masterly, a striking contrast with the sweetly timid Maggie we all knew and loved.

"I did the thing Viktor showed us," she said proudly. "I didn't just see the position; it was like I *felt* it. I can hardly wait to tell him about it.

"Maggie-san: I see that you have learned the crane kick from the infinitely wise Mister Miyagi," P.D. said.

I cracked up and was *that* close to chanting "wax on, wax off," but thought better of it: It might sound creepy, like a dirty joke. Last thing Maggie needed to hear right now.

Instead I nearly killed the mood in a different way, by blurting some unwanted advice. "Not to bust anyone's balloon, but we gotta be careful now. Next round, we'll all be paired with winners; we can't get too high on ourselves and underestimate them."

P.D. rolled his eyes. "Thanks, mom."

"He's right, though," Zamir said. "I am glad he said it, even if he sounded like a douche."

Everyone burst into laughter. Zamir looked perplexed.

"Did I say it wrong?"

"No, you said it exactly right," Esther said, grinning. "We're just pleasantly surprised to hear you talking like a Murican all of a sudden. And of course, we can all agree that Moses is a douche."

For once I was happy to take the hit. Nothing like goofing on Moses Middleton to bring people together. We were happy with each other, loose, inspirited. Ready for Round Two.

This time I drew a whippet-thin, hypertense Latino dude from William Cullen Bryant, known as one of the best publics in Queens. He was a leg-shaker, and I had to fight distraction as the table quivered, rattling the pieces. I ran the Danish, thankful that he didn't screw up my plans by responding with the Sicilian or the French. After I offered up the second pawn sacrifice with c3, which is supposed to lead to early deployment of both my bishops and a huge advantage in development, he declined to capture. Instead he pushed his queen over to e7, fixing his sights on my king and leaving his own pawn *en prise.* Unsound move, I thought, but aggressive and disconcerting. What the hell; I grabbed his pawn. Queen takes pawn, check. Blocked it with my black bishop. From that point onward on it was easy. Molested his queen with my knights, recapturing the development lead I was after. Stopped him from castling, leading to a blunder that allowed me to pin his queen with my rook. That's all she wrote. He resigned and shook hands with the same jittery, preoccupied affect he'd had throughout the game.

Strange guy, maybe a little damaged. Needless to say, a chess tournament is probably not the best place to go if you're looking for examples of robust mental health. The game has a hallowed history of weird behavior, dating back at least as far as Paul Morphy, who supposedly could only sleep if he laid out a perfect circle of women's shoes around his bed. Even so, I was seeing more and more of these slightly off-kilter kids all over my school. Most of them, I suspected, were on some kind of meds. My mom recommended pharm only as a last resort, but there were plenty of problem kids in the hands of shrinks who doled out anti-depressants like candy. Students acting out — you know, the way teenagers do — could be diagnosed with "behavioral issues" and drugged up, basically to keep them under control. P.D., the poster child for Oppositional Defiant Disorder, had scored a Ritalin scrip way back in Middle School. He never swallowed the damn things but made pocket money by selling them on in the playground. They were in high demand. And Ritalin was pretty mellow compared to the heavy-duty zombie shit that some of the kids were on.

My circle, on the other hand, was pharma-free. We bristled at teachers' dumbass diktats and had hella troubles to cope with, but — with the possible exception of P.D. — we were basically chill and had the social skills necessary to negotiate high school. Even P.D., when he had to, could put on a pretty persuasive show of being a stable, well-adjusted kid. So we'd all managed to stay clear of meddling counselors and predatory shrinks. And meds.

As the team drifted back to our table, I took stock. Incredibly, we'd all won again. Zamir totted up the scores from Bryant and Hillcrest on the back of a scoresheet. He concluded that we were leading the team competition by at least a point. As we analyzed the games, it was easy to see that our opponents had been backfooted by our coordinated aggression. And word was already getting around. Zamir reported that he'd overheard the kids from Hillcrest spilling goss about our team, the mysterious squad with matching T-shirts who were all running the same openings. Hillcrest had their super-demanding coach along; he was already drilling them on Danish and Scandy.

Came the third round. All of a sudden my nervous stomach made an appearance, quietly but persistently nudging me, whispering that the bold new Moses Middleton was a fraud. We'd be facing kids with two victories apiece and it was bound to be tough. As luck would have it, I drew a Bryant kid with a low fade and a stratospheric Elo. She had a Russian surname and this worried me somehow; I thought I might be facing a Polgar clone. I was greatly tempted to trot out French or Caro-Kann and build a careful, meticulous defense in the snorendous style to which I'd been accustomed before Viktor entered our lives. But I was committed to our team strategy, so I swallowed hard and ran the Scandinavian.

It was a catastrophe. Devotchka was completely unintimidated. She grabbed my pawn; I countered with Nf6; she advanced her king's knight and serenely ceded her king's pawn. A couple of moves later, after an exchange of bishops, she brought out her queen and suddenly I was the one on the defensive. The middle game was like a boxing match. She jabbed repeatedly; I ducked and counterpunched. Nevertheless I was holding my own — right up to the point where I executed a spectacular faceplant.

We were basically even-up, both trying to solve a wildly complex position, when I began to feel overwhelmed. I was having trouble seeing the whole board, getting distracted as I tried to pull combinations out of my ass. I was pressing and I could sense my concentration slipping. I reached into my pants pocket, hoping to renew my focus with a magic boost from the Pushkin coin. *It wasn't there.* Un. Effing. Believable. I'd left the damn thing at home. I could picture my talisman where it must have been at that very moment: lying on top of the dresser under the Campanella portrait, where I guess I'd been subconsciously building a kind of altar to Afro-descendant genius. I tried to tell myself that it was only an emotional crutch, that I didn't need it to play to my strengths. No joy. I panicked, hurried my move, blundered, losing a rook through sheer, idiotic carelessness. Just like that it was over. I was stone dead, pining for the fjords like Python's parrot. Worse, now I'd have to play it through to the bitter end, following Viktor's directive, even though Elo Girl was never going to blow a won game. The inevitable trade-down and subsequent checkmate happened mercifully quickly.

Felt like shit. On a stick. The worst part was knowing that I'd let my teammates down. Checked the results at the scorer's table: Maggie, Zamir, and P.D. had each notched another W; Esther and I were the only losers. A strong round, actually, but we were now in a dead heat with Bryant. Hillcrest was close behind. Round Four was shaping up to be a brutal struggle. Every point would count.

I should've gone straight to our table but I couldn't face my teammates just yet. I slunk outside with the idea of scoring a bag of tendies (don't tell my mom), hoping a jolt of greasy consolation would get my mind right. Instead, to my astonishment, I ran smack into Viktor. Almost literally. He was hanging on the corner, smoking one of those foul-smelling Russky cigs.

"Viktor — I mean, Mr. Fleischmann. What are you doing here?"

"To be perfectly frank, Moses, I had little to do today and I found myself drawn to this place as though by a magnet. I would be grateful if you would refrain from telling your comrades that I am here. As you know, my hope is that you will draw your strength from each other, not from me. How goes it?"

I filled him in on the overall situation and he nodded, obviously pleased.

"You have performed even better than I had hoped. It would be premature to congratulate you, but I am more than satisfied."

I explained what had me worried most of all: Maggie, Zamir, and P.D. each had three wins. The pairings algorithm was a little mysterious, but there was a very real possibility that two of those three would end up meeting each other in the final round. If that happened, as a team we could only get one point total from two of our strongest players. This would leave the whole team at a disadvantage. It wasn't hard to see that my next game was a must-win.

"I'm feeling the pressure, to put it mildly. Do you have any advice for me?"

He took a staggeringly huge hit of tobacco and exhaled sensuously. "I am reminded of Mark Twain's cat."

"I'm afraid you lost me, Mr. Fleischmann."

"Your Mark Twain was quite popular in the Soviet Union, not only because he was entertaining but also because he loved the people. He was a furious critic of capitalism and imperialism. Beyond this, he was wise in the ways of men. He once wrote, if I remember correctly: 'We should be careful to get out of an experience only the wisdom that is in it — and stop there lest we be like the cat that sits down on a hot stove lid. She will never sit down on a hot stove lid again. And that is well, but also she will never sit down on a cold one anymore.'"

"I'm not sure I get the point."

"Your opponents will perhaps draw the wrong lesson from the previous rounds. They will now be so wary of the Danish and the Scandinavian that they will seek to disrupt them, even at the cost of running openings with which they are not fully comfortable. Should you play the Danish, expect your adversary to decline. He will very soon find himself in uncertain territory. Complex positions will arise that will require you to comprehend the situation across the whole board. Remember our rotation exercise and use what you learned. And Moses: Do not forget Mr. Pushkin. You must concentrate."

Damn. Now I had to tell him how I'd freaked out in the previous round when I discovered I'd left my ruble at home. This was bound to be humiliating. He'd see me as an irredeemable buttknuckle. At the very least he'd be pissed off by my carelessness.

To my relief, however, he was quite sympathetic. He smiled, a little slyly.

"We chess players are reputed to be coldly rational beings, but in fact we are a superstitious lot. I have never been one to reject a crutch if it is helpful." He reached into his overcoat pocket and produced his cigarette case, shaking the *papirosi* into his hand. He offered the empty case to me.

"You may borrow this — placebo, shall we say? — to assist you in the last round. May it bring you good fortune. You should know that Pushkin survived numerous duels because of misfires and errant shots. He was a very lucky man — that is, until his luck ran out. Perhaps, in his final duel, he neglected to bring a talisman."

I bade him goodbye and took the case gratefully, promising not to lose it on pain of ignominious death.

His parting shot was a Russian proverb: "*Glaza boyatsa, a ruki delayut,*

Moses. This means, approximately: The eyes are afraid but the hands do."

I understood this to be a Russian version of the Nike slogan. I had to master my fears and just get on with the damn thing. As I returned to the lunchroom, I ran my fingers over the worn silver surface of Viktor's case. I could sense Pushkin's engraved features with my fingertips. Who else had touched this holy object? Tal? Petrosian? Botvinnik himself? Just as Viktor had once summoned Che, perhaps I could call on their spirits for help. I was going to need it.

13. FROM EACH ACCORDING TO HIS ABILITY

No time for tendies, so I snatched a bag of spicy ramen snacks and made it back to our table in time to analyze my Epic Fail. I could feel myself grimacing with embarrassment, but I played through that cursed game like a good soldier, resolving to own the hurldown and move beyond it. My teammates were good to me; the inevitable mockery was minimal and even a little affectionate. I almost choked up when Maggie, unasked, brought me a fistful of Pocky sticks and an energy drink from the bodega. Breakfast of Champions.

When the pairings were posted, the rush to the scorer's table was even more chaotic than usual. Zamir, who had slipped naturally into the role of team scribe, ventured forth and returned with dire news. The worst had come to pass: Zamir and P.D. were matched up in the final round. Scratch one point from our team total. I drew an East Asian kid from Flushing High who, like me, had blown his previous round. Not a superstar by any means, but potentially just as dangerous to our chances if I failed to keep my head together. We all knew the score: Maggie, Esther, and I all pretty much had to win. Maggie, perfect through three games, faced the scariest fadeup: She'd drawn Elo Girl and would be running a perma-death challenge on an unfamiliar level. We all wished each other luck and exchanged words of encouragement: a new thing for us. P.D. leered ferociously, flashed me a cod gang sign, and winked. Even Esther, who by this point in a tournament had usually lost interest, seemed to have caught the spirit. She gave me a bump.

"Get it, Mose," she said, with a look of real conviction.

"Never fear," I replied. Clearing my throat, I proceeded to Austen. (I'd found a quote on Google and had been saving it up for an occasion like this.) "My courage always rises at every attempt to intimidate me."

"Why, Moses — a lady might almost think that a gentleman has troubled himself to make an impression." She smiled, lightly brushing my shoulder with her fingertips, and cocked an eyebrow. "Evidently you have some decent qualities, despite everything." This was irony, sure, but I thought I detected some genuine warmth behind the façade.

With that, I rode into battle, feeling specially blessed, like a knight who'd received his lady's veil as a favor for the joust to come. Blame it on youthness. At some point I guessed I would need to dial back my growing feelings for Esther — before I blurted something fawkward and ruined everything — but for now I was gonna take it. And use it.

I decided to stick with the Danish. It had served me well in the earlier rounds, so I felt pretty comfortable with it by now. What I didn't anticipate was that my opponent would unleash the ultimate psychological weapon. He was, I could tell right off, that most dreaded of adversaries: a genuinely *nice guy*.

"Duuuuuude! I'm Lee." He gave me a friendly, unaffected grin as he settled down over the board. Asian guy. He *looked* like northern Queens, but he sure didn't *sound* like it. Couldn't tell if he was new in town or just jocking the movies, but he had a full-on Left Coast stoner accent.

"Awesome to make your acquaintance, bro. Let us rock." Huge cockeyed grin. "Whoa, gnarly T-shirt." His own tee depicted a clock with the hands set to 4:20 — the kind of thing that would get you sent home from school if the teachers knew what it meant. I stammered a polite response and we dapped, thumb-style.

I don't think his Jeff Spicoli routine was a deliberate tactic, but it might as well have been. His obvious warmth and goofy surfside demeanor disarmed me, like we were just hangbuds playing skittles instead of mortal enemies. Somehow I had to reclaim my killer instinct. I played e4, punched the clock, and girded for battle. Nice guy or no, I needed to smash his pumpkins.

When I offered the gambit, he didn't look fazed at all, but he thought for a good long time. A couple of minutes ticked off his clock. Eventually he grabbed my queen's pawn. I offered the second gambit with c3. Again, he pondered the board for a couple of minutes, then shrugged and declined, just as Viktor had anticipated. He launched a gambit of his own with d5. I captured; he regained the pawn with his queen. We developed pieces for a few moves and his queen ended up on e5, vectoring toward my king. He'd turned the tables on me. I didn't get the big lead in development that I'd been aiming for, and he'd taken the initiative.

A couple of moves later he managed to snatch one of my pawns, and although my position looked stronger, that lost material had me deeply worried. I needed to recalibrate my thinking about this game. No opportunity for the slashing aggression that had worked for me in my earlier Danish games; instead, I was looking at a complex dynamic that would lead to an unpredictable middle. At this point, I knew, I needed to comprehend the forces at play across the whole board, Botvinnik-style. But it wasn't coming naturally to me. My thinking was too linear, leading down blind alleys, and I could feel the seeds of panic stirring again as I contemplated the intimidating number of choices available. This time, though, I simply refused to buckle. I reached into my pocket and massaged the magic cigarette case.

If this were a movie, I thought, Alexander Sergeyevich would now materialize in the lunchroom, visible only to me of course, and dispense some critical, meme-ready nugget of wisdom. I imagined the great Russian poet holding forth in a screechy Yoda voice — "Do or do not, malchik; there is no try" — and cracked up. Suppressed a snort of laughter with only partial success; got a dirty look from the adjoining table — and instantly I was chill. Maybe this wasn't the way the talisman was supposed to work, but what the hell: It worked. I was right back in the groove, feeling relaxed and ready for action. I don't think I was truly operating in The Zone, but I was feeling whole, like a fully rational human being, with emotions in the house but appropriately regulated by reason. I no longer felt that I needed to hate my opponent; on the contrary, I began to see him as my collaborator in a complicated process that was whirring smoothly forward like a well-oiled machine.

Now I saw where the game was going. It was not going to be won by a killer combination. I needed to simplify. I would trade down, trying to gain a positional edge from each exchange. We were headed for a grandmasterish endgame, exploiting minute advantages and pushing pawns to the bitter end. Bitter end? Triumphant conclusion, rather. I was gonna make this happen for my comrades.

My man Lee seemed thoughtful and deliberate as I executed my strategy — maybe too deliberate for his own good. I happened to glance at the clock and noticed that he was in moderate time trouble. As we entered the endgame, I was still a point down but he had only a couple of minutes to burn. For the first time his mellow vibe was noticeably harshed; he drove pawns and king down the board briskly and a little nervously. Then, under pressure, he blundered, letting my pawn sneak through to an open file. Suddenly I owned the eighth rank; promotion was a slam dunk.

"Whoa, grubbed it, bro. Guess you're the better man." He offered his hand; I thanked him for the game; the point was mine. Now I had to hope that it would be enough.

Jogged back to our table, where Esther was relaxing, more or less, with phone in hand. Turned out she'd won decisively. This was the first time she'd achieved a winning overall score in any of our tournaments, as she was pleased to remind me.

"You defended our honor, nobly, like the sainted Chevalier."

This merited an eyeroll. "You're kissing ass just a little too enthusiastically today. Climb down off my leg, young man."

Burned. But hey, this was the Esther I'd always known and loved, so it didn't really hurt my soul.

P.D. and Zamir were next to arrive.

"He let me win," Zamir announced breathlessly. "He was being polite."

"Polite? Me? Never happen," P.D. responded. "It was a vicious heist, Mose. He played the Albanian gambit. Used that innocent face to distract me from his evil schemes." P.D. grinned. Ordinarily he *hated* to lose, but it looked like he didn't mind losing to our boy from the Balkans.

We did a quick assessment of the points. We were still dead even with Bryant, so everything hung on the results of Maggie's game. I felt kind of sick inside. She'd been put through the wringer over the past few weeks, and now she had to shoulder the burden for the whole team. She always seemed so fragile; I was afraid she'd break.

We scanned the lunchroom and saw that Maggie and Elo Girl were still hard at it. There couldn't be much time left on their clocks. P.D., Zamir, and I drifted over to their table; Esther held back, saying she couldn't bear to look. We hoped to ghost in silently so as not to distract them, but we needn't have bothered. The entire Bryant team, along with Hillcrest's overbearing coach, were arrayed around the board, keeping a polite distance but making their presence unmistakable to the players.

The position was stark: pawns and kings, a classic race for promotion. Maggie looked troubled; Elo Girl had a pawn lead and her victory seemed assured. This was the point where a grandmaster would resign, but Maggie was sticking with Viktor's advice and refusing to fold. Elo Girl reached the final rank and swapped her pawn for a queen. She slapped her clock with a flourish.

That's when I saw it. She had maybe a couple of seconds left on the clock, while Maggie had a full minute to burn. Elo Girl was too delighted with herself to notice. Maggie moved her king into a defensive position and punched the clock; Elo Girl swooped in to position her queen for the killing blow, but it was too late. The flag dropped. Game over. A collective groan from the Bryant kids. I actually felt sorry for them; they'd been *this* close but pegged out on a buzzer-beater. Put it in the books.

Maggie, looking happily stunned, arose from her seat, and Zamir was the first to embrace her. Esther arrived and we collapsed into a classic group hug, jumping up and down with exhilaration. Even P.D., who was way too cool for pep-rally bullshit, seemed to be jiggling a little bit on the periphery. It occurred to me that we were performing the triumphant slo-mo sequence that you'll see over the closing credits of an 80s teen flick. All we needed was some corny synth victory music. It was staggering: With Viktor's guidance, we'd gone from complete non-entities to the best in Queens — for today at least. We were becoming winner.

Only now did it cross my mind that Maggie and Zamir were now the only two entrants with perfect 4-0 scores. One of them was going to win the individual trophy, depending on an algorithm that would evaluate the strength of their opponents. Suspense. After a few minutes the awards ceremony got under way, with some Q150 teacher hamming it up like an emcee at the Grammys.

"Every one of you is a winner today." They always say that so as to throw the losers a bone; never helps when you've been buttkicked all over the building. "But we're excited to announce that the individual champion of today's tournament is — Meiling Wang!"

That was Maggie. Zamir looked delighted; he was as happy for her as if he'd won the damn thing himself. Maggie didn't react for a couple of seconds; couldn't believe what she was hearing. Esther had to steer her to the front of the hall, where she accepted a stonking great plastic trophy and posed shyly for our cell photos.

"I know I was very lucky," she told us as she rejoined the gang. "I played better than I ever have, but I'm not on a level with P.D. and Zamir."

"Don't sell yourself short, girl," Esther said. "You're the best in Queens right now. Feel it."

Vigorous noises of agreement from all. Maggie blushed but she was unmistakably chuffed. As was I, on her behalf. Nobody deserved a little sweetness more than she did just then. I tapped her on the shoulder and gestured toward the floor.

"Check it out, Maggie," I deadpanned. "A small dark oily stain." She shrieked with laughter.

After Maggie's triumph, the team trophy was almost an anticlimax. (I lie; everyone was feverish hyped). We assembled in our durfy matching T-shirts and posed with another plastic monstrosity while my new buddy Lee snapped some commemorative photos for our files.

Zamir thrust the team trophy into my arms. "You deserve this, Mose. You are the big man who made it happen."

"Nah, we all did it together. But I'll strap it to the hood of my Cadillac for the rest of the weekend. On Monday, it'll go straight into 722's trophy case. Lots of room in there."

Viktor was waiting outside, arms folded, an interrogatory eyebrow raised. Maggie filled him in with a breathless tumble of words and thanked him lavishly. She was so smacked that she threw herself into his arms and received a brief, courteous embrace in return.

"I expected nothing less, my children. Please understand that this is your victory, not mine. However, I will say this, once, before I resume my customary attitude as your stern and demanding coach: You give me a reason to get up in the morning."

Grinning like a fool, I handed Viktor the cigarette case.

"Thank you, Moses. Many believe that chess is an art, not a science. It is fitting, then, that you may attribute your victory in part to the soul of a poet."

That night I was too buzzed for sleep, so I challenged the usual array of patzers online and played like a crazed muffa until I could feel my eyelids drooping. Toddled off to bed and let my thoughts float free. Another major tournament was coming up in a couple of weeks. This time it was a citywide open; we'd be facing the genius squads from Stuyvesant and Bronx Science, not to mention all the snooty preps and privates like Galton.

Stuyvesant: damn. Whenever I thought about Stuyvesant or Bronx Science, I felt a little twinge of self-loathing. I was probably smart enough to have gotten into one of the specialized high schools, but I'd blown off the citywide exams. I'd told Mom and Dad that I wanted to stay in the neighborhood; they were dubious but they'd finally shrugged and assented after a long, excruciating family conference. The truth was, I was scared of failing the test. And the idea of *passing* the test was even scarier. I'd be thrown in among the city's smartest kids, in a school that was all about high-powered competition, and I just didn't think I was good enough to handle it. Mom always said I needed to respect myself more, give myself a chance to excel. She was probably right. Maybe if I was facing the decision today, with the confidence I was learning from Viktor, I'd give it a shot. But I'd missed my chance, and I knew I'd always regret it.

So here I was, stuck in 722 and trying to make the best of it. We'd managed to go from mediocrity to excellence in one big jump. Was it repeatable? Viktor's strategy had worked like a charm, but the element of surprise wouldn't carry us through the next tournament: The other guys would be ready for us. Our most obvious improvement was due to our newest member. Adding Zamir to the team was, of course, huge: He was seemingly as good as P.D., and 722 was always going to be stronger with two chess lords in the house. On the other hand, we couldn't count on Maggie for another sweep tbh. She'd been *unconscious* throughout the afternoon; I was psyched to see her playing over her head like that, but I doubted she'd be able to stay on that level consistently.

In the last analysis, maybe, our best chances would lie with the lower boards, like the Soviet team in that legendary USSR vs. The Rest of the World extravaganza. That stale slogan was for real: We were in this together. Esther was no superstar, but all of a sudden she cared. It wasn't just about supporting her BFF; she wanted to do her best for the rest of us, and she was going to be good for extra points every time. And me? Well, I still couldn't let go of the idea that I could elevate my game to P.D.'s level, but deep inside I knew I was at best half-mortal, like my man Hercules. I'd keep grinding, trying to absorb Viktor's teaching and push my Elo up incrementally. Maybe, just maybe, I could go 4-0 next time through; I'd been pretty damn close this afternoon.

Of one thing I had no doubt: Our biggest edge going forward was our collective spirit. All of us could contribute; every one of us had each other's back; if one or two of us stumbled, another would step forward and pick us all up. To quote another Black genius that nobody knows was Black: "All for one and one for all."

14. PERSONALITY DISORDER

Winning a tournament — winning anything — was pretty big news at 722. On Monday morning we got a shout-out from the vice principal during homeroom intercom announcements, and I was sensing a measure of respect in the hallways for a change. Got a thumbs-up from a couple of jocks; one of the pot-smoking gangsta wannabes threw up a 37th Avenue hand sign, performing a half-serious local variation on the signals used by L.A.'s legendary 38th Street gang. Marco tried to stare me down a couple of times that week but I was fairly confident that he wouldn't come at me in my hour of triumph. He was the kind of predator who thrives on weakness, and at that moment I was feeling strong.

Later in the week my dad mentioned that he'd received the C.V. from Maggie's mom. It looked pretty solid, he thought, but he wanted to meet her before sending it up the ladder. He suggested inviting her and Maggie to one of our dinners. He felt, and I agreed, that hanging out with our big shaggy extended family would be less intimidating than a one-on-one, which was bound to feel like a high-stakes interview. I texted Maggie. She was nervous that the whole thing was going to be painfully awkward, but I persuaded her that it was our best shot at getting the thing done. Me doing people management again. After a convoluted exchange of messages, we set it up for Friday evening.

Thursday was club night again, and if any of us were expecting fresh magic tricks from Viktor, we were disappointed. The gambit gimmick had worked as anticipated, cementing team solidarity and catching our opponents on the back foot. But it was unlikely to work twice, he warned us. Other teams would be boning up on Danish and Scandy; moreover, at the upcoming citywide open we'd be facing players too strong to be thrown off by non-standard openings. We would need to rely on study and discipline. He led us on a brief tour of black's opening repertoire in response to 1. d4; then shifted to a series of grueling endgame exercises. We shouldn't be sucked into an obsession with openings, he said: He'd seen too many intermediate players thrown out of synch when encountering an unexpected variation. So long as we didn't blunder, sound tactical play and control of the center could carry us through to victory regardless of the first few moves.

"Now for the bad news: You will not win this tournament. A handful of high school players in New York City have achieved Elo ratings in excess of 2200. This is often considered master level. Such players are far from invincible, but the likelihood of beating them consistently is small. Some of you may eventually reach these lofty heights, but at this stage of your development you cannot hope to overpower them."

"So what's the point?" P.D. asked.

"The point is play to the best of your abilities and to acquit yourselves honorably. You now have a reputation to uphold, and a strong finish in this tournament will show the city that your success was no fluke. In particular, you must do everything possible to prevail against opponents of comparable strength. In this way you may accumulate a team score that allows you to place among the top schools."

Esther sighed. "I have to say it. It's difficult to get motivated when you know you can't win."

"On the contrary," Viktor replied. "For you there are significant goals to pursue apart from outright victory. Allow me to suggest one."

"After last week's tournament, I received a surprising telephone call," he continued. "I was contacted by the headmaster of a private school called Galton Prep. He wished to recruit me as coach of the Galton team and suggested that I would be well compensated should I agree."

"What the *hell*?" I blurted, forgetting for the moment the gentlemanly demeanor that Viktor preferred. "How did he even *know* about you?"

Viktor chuckled. "The world of chess is New York City is small, and it thrives on gossip. I am sure that my return from Siberia, as it were, has been much discussed in the coffee houses. Presumably this Galton fellow would have made a few calls after hearing about your unexpected success in Sunnyside."

"You're not leaving us, are you?" Maggie pleaded, with a catch in her voice.

"Of course not, my dear. It is you who are my children, not those little monsters of privilege. This Galton outfit represents everything I despise. It was clear to me that this principal felt *entitled* to my services, and simply assumed that I would genuflect before the power of money and social standing. He seemed quite put out when I turned him down."

I could feel a release of tension throughout the room. Our guru was not for sale. As we were loyal to Viktor, Viktor was loyal to us.

"With this episode in mind, I would suggest to you a goal worth striving for. At our first meeting we spoke of the class enemy. That is, precisely, Galton. You must bind together with the object of finishing ahead of this exclusive club, this ruling-class incubator. Let your resentment kindle your collective will. Humiliate them. Teach them that not every shiny object they see is theirs for the taking."

I could get behind that — we all could — and fantasies of revenge over the board carried me through to next evening's blow-out dinner.

I hadn't known what to expect, what with the shady night gig and all, but Maggie's mom presented as a moderately buttoned-up, totally normal local lady in early middle age. When she arrived, with Maggie in tow, on Friday evening, she was prim and proppa in a business-y skirt and low heels, styling big nerdy glasses just like her daughter's. It was easy to imagine her at a PTA meeting or in the teller window of a bank. Her face was unreadable, and maybe a little hard, as we made introductions. I assumed she was anxious and would be playing defense until she took our measure.

Mom broke the ice, radiating warmth as she administered a welcoming hug. You could feel the affectionate vibe getting across: That mom-to-mom connection is a cultural universal.

"Mrs. Wang, I am so thrilled to meet you at last. We love Maggie; she and Moses have been close friends since Middle School and we should have had you over *years* ago."

"Please call me Lily," she replied shyly. Her Chinese name was Li-Shu, as I knew from the résumé, but like Maggie and most of the Chinese-Americans in northern Queens, she used an American-type name to smooth over interactions with English speakers. "I am honored."

Mom took her in hand and whisked her off for the traditional house tour. First-time guests sometimes found this ritual a little overwhelming. Our place was half museum, half madhouse, festooned with a dizzying array of paintings and sculptures, most of which had been contributed by a succession of artsy tenants in lieu of rent. Over the living room fireplace hung a gigantic canvas depicting a busy Harlem street scene in the style of Jacob Lawrence; in the corner was one of Julian's abstract metal sculptures, which to my eyes resembled a crucified robot. Here and there on the walls were watercolors, movie posters, and ancient photos of Mom's family going all the way back to the shtetl. Along the hallway outside my room was a fairly embarrassing series of pictures I'd drawn as a kid, including (*cringe*) one of Maggie. To see the whole house, mind you, it was usually necessary to negotiate stacks of packing boxes; somebody was always on the way in or out. Controlled chaos. The scene wasn't exactly *House Beautiful*, but it reflected the way we lived and Mom was proud of it.

I had a night off from kitchen duty, so Maggie and I retreated to my room and skittled while I played some hip-hop jazz — currently my preferred beat — on the wireless speakers. By the time we drifted back downstairs the whole gang was present, sitting in the living room and rapidly killing a bottle of red. I noted that Mrs. Wang was sitting close to Allegra and chatting quietly; they'd bonded right away, perhaps over their shared experience of making do without papers in JH. Dante was quietly strumming his guitar, a gorgeous vintage Alhambra that I'd always coveted, even though I only knew three chords. In a corner Dad was deep in conversation with Ritwik, Mallika, and Julian. The subject was probably politics; for weeks they'd all been engaged in an unending dialogue about US imperialism in the Global South. I didn't usually participate but sometimes listened in. I wanted to learn about this stuff and found that I understood more from eavesdropping on their sharp (but friendly) disagreements than from I did from reading all those boilerplate pundits online.

Dinner followed, along with another couple of bottles. Mom had made a huge pot of her special mushroom risotto made with sushi rice, one of my favorites. With Mrs. Wang's permission, Maggie and I were each treated to about half an inch of the red stuff. This was in keeping with Mom's conviction that alcoholism was less common in Europe because people there didn't make a BFD about booze. It went straight to Maggie's head and she had a giggle fit, out of embarrassment I guess, when everybody congratulated her on her tournament victory. At one point she leaned over and whispered in my ear: "Mose, I wish everyone could have a family like yours. No wonder you're so happy."

This threw me: I never thought of myself as particularly happy; I was rarely felt *un*happy but I was always worried about something, always under some kind of pressure. It had never really occurred to me to think about whether I was a happy guy. I wondered if maybe that was the whole point: It's only when you're depressed that you contemplate the sad state of your psyche; otherwise, you're just cruising ahead on automatic, dealing with obstacles when they come your way, leaving the soul-searching to philosophers and emos. Maybe that's what happiness is: not perpetual bliss — though ideally you'll score a dose of mad glee now and again — but a kind of unconscious contentment that rolls along quietly in the back of your mind when nothing in particular is making you miserable.

I must have zoned out for a few seconds while I gnawed at my Deep Thought of the Day. Maybe I was feeling the effects of that thimbleful of wine. Next thing I knew Maggie was giving me a little poke in the ribs.

"Earth to Moses: Activate your Pushkin ruble. You're drifting away."

I snapped back to consciousness, surveyed the table, saw that dinner was winding up. Mrs. Wang had to work, so she thanked us all cordially and steered Maggie to the door. Allegra gave her a sisterly hug on the way out and she smiled broadly. I was jazzed; felt like the evening had been a slam dunk.

Dad had wash-up duty; I pitched in so I could ask him for a reading.

"She's a strong candidate for a job at my lab," he said. "Her English is very good and she has the right qualifications. I'd hire her in a second. Hopefully my boss will agree. More to the point, I like her, and I'm pretty sure she liked us too. She had no difficulty mind-melding with the Middleton mob."

It struck me that Dad hadn't just been giving Mrs. Wang an audition when he asked her over. He wanted her to feel our support, to be enveloped for one night in the warmth, and wackiness, of our household. Mission accomplished. Later I checked in with Maggie and she told me that her mother had seemed cheerfully buzzed on the way home; she had felt welcome and, crucially, empowered by the experience. Her confidence showed signs of returning. Most important — and Maggie choked up a little when she said it — it had been literally years since her mom had spent a pleasant evening out. This blew my mind but I could see that it must be true.

The following afternoon the club got together to take in a movie, honoring Viktor's desire that we build our solidarity through social activities that had nothing to do with chess as such. P.D., the habitual loner, had been hard to persuade, but when I discovered a revival of *Last House on the Left* in a Village rep house he signed on. He loved the horror genre and maintained that low-budget flicks of the 1970s had raised splatter to the level of art. (This particular movie, my dad informed me, was loosely based on Ingmar Bergman's *Virgin Spring*, so maybe P.D. was onto something.)

As it turned out, this might not have been the ideal choice of film. It wasn't fun horror; it was grim horror, raw and downbeat. Maggie couldn't relate and spent most of the evening with her hands covering her eyes. Esther was simply *appalled* and made me promise that the next movie we took in together had to be a full-on frock flick with uppa-class accents. P.D. volunteered that he'd be willing to catch a violence-free movie so long as there was plenty of sex; Esther promised bodice-ripping. I felt terrible but we hashed it all out successfully via a lively convo on the No. 7 train home; I was pretty sure I'd been forgiven when Esther Austened me: "Stupid men are the only ones worth knowing, after all."

We managed to recapture the mood with dinner in the Heights. Zamir entertained us with Albanian jokes, most of which made little sense to the rest of us but were hilarious anyhow because they came off so cryptic and awkward in English. The riddles translated best.

"How do you stop an Albanian tank? You shoot the soldier who is pushing it."

As we left the diner, still laughing, P.D. and I peeled off to walk Maggie home; things could get dicey in Corona after dark. We dropped her off and ambled down the block toward the bougie territory, chewing over *Last House* and rating our favorite Wes Craven joints. All of a sudden we heard rapid footsteps behind us and wheeled around in a defensive posture. It was Chen, materializing from the shadows like a cheap horror shock effect.

"Which one of you is Moses?" he demanded.

Various responses cycled through my head — the traditional "what's it to you?" sprang to mind — but I just nodded and waited for the payoff.

Fuming, he did his best to strike a threatening pose and pointed his finger at my chest. "You stop messing in family business. *Now.* And leave Maggie alone. Or I will find you and kick your ass." (Here I'm omitting about ten F-words that he dropped for emphasis.)

It wasn't hard to figure out what was happening here. Doubtless he'd heard about our dinner with Mrs. Wang; he was just the type of sociopath who'd be snooping on Maggie's phone and reading the messages. Our attempt to reach out to his sister-in-law was bound to be a threat to him; he liked things just fine the way they were, with him dominating the household through a kind of domestic terror. Damn. I'd found myself in the midst of yet another knife-edge confrontation. That's growing up in New York City, I guess. One day you're reading *Captain Underpants* and learning to color inside the lines; the next, you're handling street altercations with thugs, perverts, and deranged yuppies.

At my shoulder I could sense P.D. vibrating, seething with rage. His alleged personality disorder was in full effect. In another instant he exploded into action. It was hypersonic, violent, shocking: He uncoiled like a torsion spring and seized Chen's arms, pinning him against the plexiglass wall of a bus shelter. He got right up in Chen's face, literally nose-to-nose, and addressed him in a slow, hushed voice that conveyed infinitely greater threat than Chen's tough-guy bluster.

"Listen to me, you feeble excuse for a creepy clown. Maggie goes where she wants and sees who she wants. I am *personally* guaranteeing this. And by the way, if I ever hear that you've laid a hand on her, I'm going to put you in the frickin' ICU."

I thought I'd need to step in and break it up before something terrible happened, but I could hear a vehicle cruising toward us on the quiet. I knew that sound: NYPD Impala on patrol. We all loosened up and backed off as 5-0 rolled past, freezing us in the beam of a tactical response flash and growling at us on the P.A.

"Everything groovy here, citizens?"

Great. A cop who thought he was a comedian. But we had to worry: From his point of view, we were two suspish non-white adolescents accosting an older dude. This was the kind of hectic situation that could escalate fast, leaving young brown bodies bleeding on the sidewalk.

"It's fine, officer. These my friends," Chen said. He had no more wish to tangle with the cops than we did. We all flashed shit-eating grins, opened our hands, and made what we hoped were innocent-sounding noises.

"Okay, get your asses off the street. I see you again tonight, you're spending the night in the precinct. Peace out, kiddies." He popped an ear-splitting siren blast and fanged off. Chen booked without another word. It occurred to me that we'd carried out Mallika's recommendation without forethought. I could only hope that she had been right — that P.D.'s brand of charismatic menace would keep Chen in his cage for a while.

As far as I knew, nobody had hipped P.D. to Chen's pervy machinations, but he had powerful antenna for detecting abuse — I'd have to ask him about that someday — and he'd intuited the situation by reading the dynamics between Maggie and her uncle. He was breathing hard; slowly the fiery blaze in his eyes died down and he wrapped himself once more in his protective mantle of *cool.*

"You okay, friend?" I asked.

"Never better, comrade. But I'm impressed by the sheer number of dudes who are lining up to take a piece out of you. I should sell tickets."

He gave me a farewell bump and I stood for a while and watched him as he faded into the darkness, fully self-contained, completely alone.

15. FRIENDLY FASCISM

Next day I checked in with Maggie via SMS to see whether there had been repercussions following that freaky confrontation with Chen. Nothing major, I was relieved to learn. He'd stormed in a few minutes after she got home, slamming doors and making angry noises while she cowered in her room. But he'd left her alone and eventually passed out in front of the tube. Maybe Mallika had been right. P.D.'s mad-dog mode was super-intimidating; with luck, it would keep Pervy Uncle on ice for a few beats.

The week flew by as I girded my loins, Herc-style, for Saturday's tournament. Meanwhile there was hopeful news from my dad. He'd spoken to his boss and shared the résumé. She was enthusiastic and promised to set up an interview. As Dad had anticipated, she saw this as a point of principle and was more than ready to give Mrs. Wang an opportunity, one that would otherwise be unavailable to an immigrant in her situation. He promised to give me the word the instant he heard anything.

A couple of days later — must have been Wednesday morning — P.D. and I had lined up a meet, squeezed in as usual between periods, for a clandestine vaping session by the dumpsters. He was late, and when he showed he looked weirdly shaken. As he fired up his mod I tried to make conversation.

"You psyched for tonight's club meeting, son?"

"How I'm feeling is immaterial, I regret to say. I won't be there."

"C'mon, P.D. Don't mess with me. We need you. And it's no fun if you're not around."

"No, I mean I can't do it. Literally. This morning I got called in to face the firing squad. For truancy. The disciplinary committee, in their infinite wisdom, has banned me from all extracurricular activities for the rest of the semester. That means no club and no tournament."

"WTF? That's frickin' outrageous. Your attendance has been pretty good lately, especially since Viktor came on the scene. I don't get it."

P.D. shrugged. "You know that new vice principal lady? Doctor Evil? She's got me in her gunsights. Seems she doesn't like my *attitude.* It's entirely up to her whether I get reinstated. In the meantime, I'm Cool Hand Luke. If I step out of line in any way, the Boss is going to put me in the hole. They can harass my folks, do an investigation, file something called a 407 Form. They can even refer me to Juvie. If I stick around for this bullshit, I'm going to be walking the tightrope for the rest of the semester."

I knew nothing about P.D.'s situation at home. I didn't have the impression that he was being raised by the Huxtables. Still, I had to ask.

"What about your family? Can they do something?

"My naïve young friend: I don't really have a family, not in any traditional sense. Mom took off years ago. Pop's a drunk; hasn't worked in months. They can call him up all they want, send him scary-looking official notices; he won't do anything about it. I'm completely on my own here."

"But there's gotta be some way out of this. Get you a lawyer or something."

"Yeah, right. Even if anyone gave a shit, which I doubt, ain't nobody gonna work for free. In the meantime, comrade, I am most decidedly outta here. They might as well expel me. School is going to be unbearable under these conditions."

He pocketed his mod and pulled out a pack of Kools.

"Observe, Mose-man. Real smoke. If I'm going to be pigeonholed as a juvenile delinquent, I might as well act like one."

He blazed the nail, threw jazz hands, and danced away down the sidewalk, singing in a voice laced with bitter irony.

"When you're a threat, you're a threat all the way, from your first cigarette to your last dying day."

I stood there boggled, completely sketched out. My throat tightened. Sure, my chess dreams had been blown out of the water, but what was happening to my friend was far worse than any disappointment over a board game. I felt clueless, powerless, kneed in the nads. Then I remembered Volonté's epitaph: "*Non aveva paura di niente, ha osato tutto.*" I had to do *something*, or at least try.

At my next break I went straight to Sanprudencio's office. A bored-looking assistant buzzed her; at first she claimed she was too busy to see me. I begged — literally begged — for five minutes of her time. She gave in. Sort of.

In the event, it was five minutes of relentless gaslighting, delivered in phrases poached from the EduSpeak Manual. I took a seat in front of her oversized executive desk, where she displayed herself under an enormous Frida Kahlo poster that screamed 'woke.' She started right in, even before I could open my mouth. I wasn't helping, she said. P.D. was a troubled young man in need of tough love. My responsibility was to "motivate his progress" and to "model appropriate behaviors"; meanwhile she would provide "formative assessments" to track his progress as he learned "developmental best practices." She accused me of valuing the chess club over my friend; managed to hint that the club's continued existence would be conditional on my continuing cooperation. She dismissed me curtly and swiveled to her computer monitor, her back to my face. I hadn't managed to utter a single word. Drifted through the rest of the day's classes in a state of impotent rage, fantasizing revenge and hating myself for my weakness.

At dinner Dad couldn't help noticing how dejected I was.

"Mose, you've got a face like a wet weekend. Anything you can share with the gang?"

Ordinarily I hated to burden everyone with my problems, but I thought maybe I'd feel better if I could get this off my chest. I swallowed hard and spilled the whole sad story.

"Can't P.D. just be sure to show up from now on?" My mom asked, reasonably enough. But the situation was not reasonable.

"This vice principal is a major gaslighter and she's vindictive as hell. Everybody assumes that she has an enemies list. She'll hound him; make his life unbearable. Dr. Sanprudencio brooks no resistance."

Dante looked up with a curious expression on his face.

"Mose, did you say Sanprudencio? That's a very unusual name."

I nodded. "Yeah, Stacey Sanprudencio. I assume it's some kind of Spanish saint?"

"Must be. But this is weird. You know a few years back I did a semester at Hunter School of Education. I was playing with the idea of getting a certificate. Thought maybe I could teach music in the schools. Didn't work out."

Dante could cook like a master chef but he hated restaurant work. It was just something he did to put food on the table while he tried to make it as a musician. Teaching music to kids would have been a decent compromise, I guess; I was sorry to hear that nothing had come of it.

"The reason I ask is that I knew a very, um, *unusual* woman at Hunter called Anastasia Sanprudencio. I wonder if it's the same person."

"Let me check it out online," I offered. "Shouldn't be too hard to find out."

I pulled out my phone and summoned her LinkedIn page. Bingo.

"Definitely the same," I said. "Full name: Anastasia Sanprudencio. Has a master's from Hunter Ed." Couldn't help laughing as I scrolled through her profile. "Damn, she's woke. Too woke to joke. Her profile is, like, the epitome of political correctness."

"Well, *that's* a surprise," Dante said. "The girl I knew at Hunter was an outspoken right-winger. Came from a wealthy family of white anti-Castro Cubans. Always organizing on behalf of CIA-sponsored coups and Color

Revolutions in Latin America. Coming from Guatemala, I'm super-sensitive to that kind of bullshit. Word: She was pretty openly racist. Could be very interesting to check out her Twitter from a few years ago."

Mallika spoke up. "Mose, social media is a new frontier in my practice. If you find anything, let me know. I might have some ideas about how we could use it."

After dinner I set to work at the laptop. Had to use snooping skills that I'd honed back in Middle School when I was coping with some online bullying. Nothing came easy. Her Facebook entry was squeaky clean. Tried a bunch of different searches on Twitter using every possible variation of her name, with bits of biographical data thrown in. No joy. Then I tried YouTube and hit paydirt. She'd given a speech at a college rally in opposition to the Venezuelan government. The clip itself wasn't all that damning, but it gave me a lead. The metadata included a social media handle: @freedomfighta59. Switched back to Twitter; pulled up an old account with the same name. It was her. The profile pic was unmistakable, a younger, slimmer version of Doctor Evil, plus there was plenty of detail in her tweets that confirmed who she was.

The account looked like it hadn't been touched in years, but there was a lot of old stuff still accessible. I paged back till I was looking at posts from her undergraduate days at CUNY. It was mostly typical college stuff — event announcements, complaints about food, inside jokes with friends. Nothing that reflected what Dante remembered about her. Then it occurred to me that she might have sanitized her timeline. So I pulled up one of the sites where old tweets get archived, wondering if I might be able to find some posts that she'd deleted.

I found them all right. *Holy shit.* It was nauseating. I felt like Maggie at the movies, afraid of what I might see and peeking between fingers to catch a glimpse of the horrors onscreen. First off, I noticed that she favored the N-word. A *lot.* She used the spelling with an "a" on the end, like white hipsters do when they're trying to imply that they're cool enough to be down with Black folk. Made me shudder. It's hard to think of a situation more humiliating than coping with white acquaintances who try to establish credibility with phony hiphop Ebonics. That ain't micro-aggression; it's full-on *aggression.* Whether they're conscious of it or not, they're sending you a message that the price of social acceptance is condoning their racist bullshit and pretending they're honorary bruthas. What they're really demanding is the shuck and jive. Nobody here but us chickens, massa.

The N-word tweets were bad enough, but the really poisonous stuff could be found in a few threads about immigration. Her view, openly expressed, was that Asians, Latin Americans, and Africans were a bunch of freeloaders who came to the US to live on welfare while breeding huge, parasitical families. She hated Afro-Cubans most of all. There was a sick-making thread quoting various "experts" who had supposedly proved the genetic inferiority of Afro-descendants to wypipo. They were a permanent underclass, lazy and criminally inclined, with low IQs and overactive sex drives. My dad had warned me that there was a big demand in academics for this kind of bogus research, but I hadn't really seen it before. It was straight-up hate, hiding behind a thin veneer of scientific-sounding weasel words. None of this recycled garbage could be excused as youthful indiscretions on her part. She'd been a fully grown adult; she knew exactly what she was doing. It was unacceptable, I was sure, that such a person now held sway over a student body that was mostly immigrants and non-whites.

I screen-capped everything and saved it to a file. Wrapped it up in a zip and pushed it over to Mallika. She texted me almost immediately.

>*This woman must be stopped. Will play some hardball. Keep confidential for now. Stay tuned.*

I'd stay tuned all right, but I didn't have high hopes. Sanprudencio represented everything I hated about high school. We called it "friendly fascism." The administrators wanted to control every aspect of your life, and they'd perfected the sinister art of pushing you around with a smile and a handshake — or these days, maybe an awkward high-five. Every oppressive measure they took was rebranded with some warm, fuzzy euphemism. Just for instance, last semester they'd introduced a whole new rulebook with a bunch of intrusive policies — like giving themselves the ability to discipline you for shady shit you did off-campus on your own time. When they rolled out the revised regs and expanded punishments, the first thing we noticed was that they'd changed the name from *Disciplinary Code* to *Community Support Guidelines*. (Wow, thanks so much for your *support*, boss.) We had no rights. Everything that made going to school worthwhile was now called a 'privilege,' meaning that they could take it away any time they felt like it. Plus in practice, the discipline was enforced arbitrarily. You could go for months without anybody noticing you were alive. Then suddenly you'd get on somebody's shitlist and you'd be terrorized, stuck in the kind of perpetual hell that was now in store for P.D. I thought about Viktor's love for the collective spirit and realized just how easily it could be exploited and twisted by petty, vindictive bureaucrats. Especially in my neighborhood, with its tradition of community activism. You couldn't walk down the block in JH or Astoria without running smack into some "socialist" politician who was actually doing dirty work for real estate developers.

Next evening at the club meeting it fell to me to give everyone the bad news. I was borderline choked up as I told the story; felt like I was delivering a eulogy. Everyone was appalled and demoralized; Maggie burst into tears. Viktor's face clouded over and he spat out a string of Russian words that had to be an elaborate curse.

Zamir, always focused on the positive side of things, spoke up. "Is there anything we can do to fix this, Mr. Fleischmann?"

Viktor sighed deeply, his lungs faintly rattling with the residue of several hundred thousand Slavic coffin nails.

"I could try the direct approach. I would be happy to schedule a meeting with this vice principal and make an appeal if you think it might help."

"With respect, Mr. Fleischmann, I think that would be a bad idea," I said. "She's not the type who can be reasoned with." I recounted the five-minute fiasco in her office. "She has a monstrous ego. Any kind of challenge to her authority just makes her want to double down. I could easily imagine her retaliating by banning you from the school."

"I know this type, I am sorry to say," Victor said. "I have told you stories of my encounters with authority in the Soviet Union. I was fortunate: For the most part, my superiors acted in good faith and in accordance with the needs of the people. I sometimes chafed at the restrictions imposed upon me, but I nearly always felt that by submitting, I was acting in aid of something more important than my own immediate preferences. However, I will not pretend that the USSR did not have problems with incompetent, power-hungry officials. Indeed we were notorious for it. Irrational bureaucracy was a tradition inherited from Czarist Russia. As a result, the Party was infested with self-serving wind-up tyrants like your Sanprudencio. True communists tried to thwart and replace such people, but it was not easy."

"How did *you* handle it?" I asked.

"One could sometimes go over their heads. A crafty appeal to self-interest could also be effective." He raised an eyebrow. "Failing that, one might try blackmail. People of this kind nearly always have something to hide."

"Actually I may have a little something cooking on the blackmail front," I said. "But I'm not counting on success. I guess we have to soldier on without P.D.; find a way to beat Galton."

Esther looked up with a defeated expression. "That's a problem, Mose. We were motivated to humiliate those guys because they're the class enemy, right? But now it turns out that our school is as evil as theirs, though in a different way. So what are we fighting for?"

"My dear Esther," Viktor replied, "ask first what you are fighting against. Nothing has changed. The enemy is the same. The enemy is *always* the same. Why are these malevolent administrators installed in your school? It is, in the end, because the parents and alumni of ruling-class institutions like Galton insist upon it. They regard you as beasts to be herded and penned. For this reason they have placed security cameras in your halls and stationed policemen at your door, have they not?"

We nodded.

"This does not happen by accident. It is of course inconceivable that such oppressive measures would be applied to the precious young scholars of Galton Prep. The class enemy is powerful enough to exert pressure on public schools, turning them, step by treacherous step, into prisons. Meanwhile the Galton children are able to attend school free of oppression. They will grow up to become untroubled adults, accustomed to the idea that they are deserving of privilege, while you — the working class — must learn and toil in an environment of surveillance and regimentation. This, I think, should constitute sufficient reason to annihilate them."

Okay, maybe this was straight-up Commie propaganda, like something out of an old movie, but I could dig it. Made sense of what was happening at 722 and similar schools across the borough. When my parents told me stories of their years in New York City publics, I was sometimes shocked by how easygoing and enjoyable their education had been. They'd been allowed — encouraged, even — to have fun. In subsequent decades, things got a little more gruesome every year. We students were the boiling frogs; it happened gradually enough that we barely noticed the changes from day to day. But by now there was no escaping the carceral gloom; we felt manipulated, put upon and nervous all the time.

Well, screw that. Viktor was right. I looked around the room and sensed that everyone else felt the same way. We were pissed and getting pumped up all over again, fortified with resentment, the OE40 of the soul.

"As for our comrade P.D. — we will find a way to fight for him," Viktor added. "In the meantime, allow me to quote a line from one of the greatest songs of the anti-fascist struggle: *Ami, si tu tombes, un ami sort de l'ombre à ta place.* It means, 'Friend, if you fall, another rises from the shadows to take your place.' You are no longer a random assemblage of individuals who can be picked off one by one. You are a team. You will press onward. They will not stop you."

Spontaneously I thrust my hand toward the center of our table and, one by one, my teammates reached out to take it. Corny? Maybe, but the press of flesh felt powerful, like we were transmitting the energy of our mutual support and — dare I say it? — affection.

"We're gonna hand Galton its overprivileged ass, am I right?"

Everyone nodded, producing hoots and other noises of agreement. Maggie, no longer tearful, surprised me by delivering a mild swear: "*Damn* right." We uncoupled, leaned back into our seats, and turned toward Viktor. He was smiling.

"You make me proud, my children. Now let us prepare."

He had us pair off and play progressive chess, a crazy variant in which white plays one move, black plays two, white plays three, and so on. His idea was to force us to look ahead — *way* ahead — both offensively and defensively. It worked, after a fashion: I was matched with Maggie, and after a couple of turns I was channeling Bobby Fischer. A few more turns and I felt like my head was going to explode. Next he introduced us to the resignations exercise. He selected grandmaster games that ended by resignation, set up the final position, and asked us to play them through to checkmate. He chose games in which the reason for resignation wouldn't necessarily be apparent to an intermediate player; he wanted us to grasp why the GM, looking ahead, could see that his position was hopeless. As always with Viktor's drills, it was about transcending linear thinking and grasping the essence of the dynamics at play.

Just when it was getting really interesting the janitor appeared at the door and cleared his throat; it was time to vacate.

Maggie, looking a little nonplussed, raised her hand.

"Mr. Fleischmann, won't you be giving us a team strategy for the tournament — like last time, when we all played Danish and Scandinavian?"

"That, my dear, was a bit of a gimmick, though it proved to be a highly effective one. This time you will be facing more sophisticated opponents, strong players who will be less likely to be disconcerted by extreme aggression, and therefore that approach is not advisable. I do, however, have a strategy to suggest. Consider that we are creatures of habit and we all have favorite openings. They make us feel comfortable, and we find ourselves relying on them — perhaps to a fault. Your best-loved openings may not in fact be your most powerful ones."

"By this time, you all know each other's strengths and weaknesses very well. Meet online. Each of you should advise his or her comrades, from the point of view of a frequent opponent, which openings they play best. You may be surprised by what you learn. Beyond this, I would advise you to adopt the classic tournament approach, which is justified by the level of competition at this event. Play aggressively with white, conservatively with black. Do not play for the draw but wait for opportunities to arise and exploit them mercilessly."

Rolled up the board; stowed the sets; accompanied Viktor to the sidewalk, where with evident relief he fired up a *papirosa.*

"By the way, you might see me at this tournament," he said as he waved goodnight. "Old friends of mine will be there and I plan to stop by and say hello. And perhaps I will have reason to boast of your prowess."

We set up a group chat for nine o'clock that evening. I tried to recruit P.D. — not even the nefarious Dr. Evil had the power to isolate him online — but he was unreachable. It felt weird to be gathering without P.D.'s grisly avatars and ironic banter. The chat turned into an impromptu group therapy session as we aired our outrage and discussed ways of coping with the loss of our comrade.

"Does this mean we cannot be the Furious Five anymore?" Zamir asked.

"Hell, no," I replied. We'll *always* be the Furious Five. P.D.'s one of us, no matter what the friendly fascists say. And we're more furious than ever."

Then Esther, looking vexed, called me out.

"Moses: You dropped a hint about some kind of shakedown in the works. Elucidate the trick bag, bwah."

"I can't just yet. I've been sworn to secrecy. Plus I don't want to get anyone's hopes up; it's a half-court heave at best. Bear with me, milady, I implore you."

She sighed and assented, provisionally at any rate.

"Okay, Mose. But I warn you, you're trying my patience."

"No Austen this time?"

"None of this tawdry bullshit rises to Jane's level, I'm afraid. You might find a more appropriate response to Dr. Sanprudencio's machinations on the men's room walls at 722."

We all promised each other we'd fix the situation somehow, not really believing it, and moved on to Viktor's request. We discussed our experiences of one another's strengths. Zamir advised me in no uncertain terms to stick with the tedious old French Defense on black, and to get serious with the super-aggressive Blackmar-Diemer gambit on white; these openings, he said, had given him the biggest headaches when playing me. We took turns commenting; each of us learned something; all of us ended up with some kind of strategic approach to Saturday's Chessapalooza. By the time we signed off, we were as ready as we could be under the circumstances. With P.D. out of action, somebody would need to arise from the shadows. Maybe it would be me.

16. I AM LEGEND

Arriving home from school Friday night I walked straight into that most dreaded of events, the family meeting. Mom and Dad beckoned me solemnly into the living room, where they were kicking off their weekend with a couple of glasses of *vin ordinaire* and a platter of painfully healthy veggie *hors d'oeuvres.* (Excuse my French.) Unshouldered my backpack and oozed reluctantly into one of our yard-sale armchairs. Was this the end of Rico? I was clueless. Major and minor transgressions whirled in my head. Had their network of nosy friends informed them about the fracas with Chen? My illicit vaping? My semi-secret caffeine habit? Did I leave my bike out in the rain or, worse, traces of pee on the toilet seat? I figured I was screwed, one way or another.

Dad opened the conversation by calling me "son," which meant we were about to discuss something of serious import. Uh-oh.

"I have some very good news and some possibly bad news."

Intriguing. I swallowed hard as Mom passed me a plate of limp carrot sticks with some kind of yoghurt dressing. Plus a glass of spring water: No wine for Moses tonight.

"Here's the good news. My boss loved Mrs. Wang and offered her a job on the spot. As I anticipated, it's an entry-level research admin position, but there's a possibility of advancement over time. In a couple of years she could end up doing hands-on science."

"Wow, kickass. What about the green card problem?"

"My boss is all over it. She's taking it personally. She and Mallika are going to conference about how to handle the immigration stuff, and I have a very good feeling about it. They will use every possible tactic either to secure the green card or to delay the process so long that it becomes moot. Those two operating in partnership are going to be formidable as hell."

"Sounds great, for sure — but don't leave me in suspense. Hit me with the bad news before I freak out and pop an aneurysm."

Dad sighed, settled back, and threw an arm around my mom's shoulders.

"I'll take this on, Al," Mom interjected. "Mose, Mrs. Wang called Allegra in tears. I guess she was embarrassed to talk to us directly. She desperately wants the job but she ran some numbers and the salary isn't enough to cover her debt payments, especially with Chen leeching money. She's devastated. She can't refinance the loan because she's undocumented, and in any case she doesn't have any real collateral."

I dropped an F-bomb, which made my parents cringe, but in this case they let it slide. They probably felt, as I did, that was the only appropriate response to a hideously messed-up situation.

"Isn't there anything we can do?"

Dad took over. "Well, yes, Moses. We have a proposal. But what we're thinking about impacts you, and we're going to need your advice and consent to proceed."

Well, this was unexpected. Suddenly they were treating 14-year-old Moses Middleton like a grown-ass adult. I leaned forward and listened hard.

"Here's the deal, Mose. Between your mom and me we think we can scrape together just enough cash to pay off Mrs. Wang's debt. Plus Dante, Ritwik, and Julian all offered to contribute some, which was a pretty remarkable gesture — if you'll excuse the phrase, they don't have a pot to piss in between them. Anyhow, if we pool the cash, we can make her an informal, interest-free loan. Off the books and person-to-person. She could retire her high-interest debt and pay us back at a monthly rate that she can afford."

"So what's the problem? Let's do it."

"This is where you come in, Mose," Mom said. "What worries us is that we'd need to dip deep into your college fund to make this happen."

"Damn, I didn't even know I had a college fund."

"You do, and it's very important to the family. When you were born, your father and I committed ourselves to making sure you'd have options 18 years down the road. Basically, we didn't want you to have to settle for CUNY if you had a chance to go to Columbia."

"Not that there's anything wrong with CUNY," Dad put in. "I learned a lot there and they did right by me. Who knows? You might even prefer it. On the other hand, you just might have an opportunity to get a degree that would write you a lifetime golden ticket. If that is your choice, we want you to be able to follow through."

"By now we've got a substantial chunk of money in the bank," Mom continued. "It won't pay your way through an Ivy school, but it means you won't be saddled with crippling debt when you graduate. It's what they call a nest egg, I guess — it represents a lot of nickels and dimes saved up over the years. It's one of the reasons we haven't accumulated all the ephemeral stuff that most families do."

I deposited "ephemeral" in my vocab bank and tried not to think too hard about the things Mom and Dad must have given up on my behalf. They weren't the type to go for resort vacations or cosmetic surgery. Bling was not their thing. But they sure could use a decent set of wheels instead of the ancient Nissan Versa that my dad struggled to keep in working order. And I knew how much Mom would've loved to baff up and dine out in Manhattan every once in a while.

Dad poured himself another modest glass of wine and leaned forward intently, hands on knees.

"So here's the pitch. By making this loan, we'd be putting our hopes for your future on the line. We think we can trust Mrs. Wang, but we need your okay. You'd be making a bet that she's going to be willing and able to make the payments. You have to be absolutely certain that it's worth the risk. Think hard about this. If you want time to mull it over, let us know."

But I'd already decided. Life was handing me an opportunity to stand up for my friend and teammate in a way that truly counted, and I wasn't going to run from it

"The answer is yes. Yes I will, yes."

Dad frowned slightly.

"Let's not rush things. I hate to make this even more difficult, Moses, but I'd like to hear your reasoning. I want to make sure you've thought it through before we make a move." This was typical of Dad, so I was ready to go.

"It's all about trust, right? I don't know Mrs. Wang very well — yet — but I'm totally sure of one thing. She will do anything to make things right for Maggie, and she will not let us down. I know I can trust her because I believe in a mother's love for her kid."

Mom actually blushed. "As you know very well, that's an argument that's bound to win me over."

"And I'm equally glad to hear it, Mose" Dad said. "I don't need to tell you that this family doesn't operate like a bank or some other soulless institution looking to squeeze profit out of every situation. Those vampires simply assume that their clients are just like them, out to screw or be screwed. So they cover their asses above all else. That's where collateral comes in. Maybe most people would think we're crazy to make a loan without it, but our asses will remain proudly uncovered. In this case, trust is the collateral."

This whole trust thing was kind of new to me, I'll admit. I'm a New Yorker; I grew up figuring that everyone was looking to get an edge on me, to find a way to take advantage. And obviously it's true of a lot of people. But what I'd learned over the past few weeks was turning my head around. I'd experienced the power of working as a team, all for one and one for all. We trusted one another implicitly, and it made us strong. Together my comrades and I could accomplish things that we could never do as individuals, out for ourselves alone and wary of everyone else. Sure, you take a risk when you trust somebody, but in a way that's the whole point. So: no fear. I didn't want my life to be shaped by suspicion and doubt. I was ready to jump into the deep end.

"Done," I said. "Let's call Mrs. Wang and close the deal. Stat. Cuz frankly, I'm hungry as hell and carrot sticks just aren't doing it for me."

Mom arose from the sofa and struck a pose. "You dine on the food of mortals, Hercules, but should I grant you entrance to Olympus you could feast on nectar and ambrosia."

"Pot roast and potatoes will do me just fine, thanks. I can smell it now, great seer."

We had a big blissful dinner, yammering at each other across the table, culminating in a toast to ourselves in celebration of the deal we were going to offer Mrs. Wang. I was so giddy with the good news that I couldn't even be bothered to worry about the tournament next day.

That evening in my room I pinged P.D. in every possible way: texted him, DM'd him on Twitter, even checked the various chess sites to see whether he was lurking. Nada. I was pretty worried about him but I reminded myself that there was precisely jack shit I could do about the situation, for now at any rate. I had to keep hoping that Mallika would be able to pull something off. To settle my nerves I played far too many games online and ended up crawling into bed after midnight.

I knew I had to catch some winks or I'd be meat at the tournament. Deployed a variety of tactics from my get-drowsy arsenal, some of which I'd been relying on since grade school. Pretended my bed was a spaceship floating past the rings of Saturn. Did some mental math tricks. Thought about girls. None of it worked.

As a last resort, I ran some scenes from Herc movies in my head. It was almost scary how accurately I remembered them. Eventually I found myself drifting, musing about why I was so fascinated by that ancient slab of muscle. I remembered what my lit teacher always says: Never take a good story at face value; try to figure out what it really means, on a deeper level. It's those underlying meanings that speak to us across centuries and borders. That's why some stories never die. We feel them. They tell us something that we know is true and important.

Then it hit me: Hercules is not just some lone, musclebound superhero out for individual glory. What he is, on a symbolic level, is everyone. The people. Us. His labors are our labor. The stories reflect the work that real people had to do in order to build a society, together, out of nothing: clear the land of wild animals, tame horses, hunt for food, even — to put it bluntly — clean up all the shit from the places we work and live.

As sleep descended, Professor Middleton reached the conclusion that Hercules' legendary strength stands for the power of shared human labor. That's why he's always refusing immortality in those campy movies. He needs to stay human because he stands for humanity as a whole. The myth, and my obsession, were finally beginning to make sense. I might not have a bitchin' set of boulders or a V-taper, but Hercules was my brother. His story was my story: the only legendary hero who's remembered primarily for working his ass off.

17. CLASS STRUGGLE

Tournament day. We had our goofy T-shirts. We had our mission. We had each other. But we didn't have P.D. Over the board we were a much weaker team without our homegrown genius, but what was worse was the feeling of incompleteness. I felt as though I was trying to sprint with a limb missing. But I knew we had to hang together, absorb our loss, and move forward with fierce resolve if we were going to have any chance of besting the Galtonites.

I arrived neurotically early, reasoning that I could use the time to scope out the scene before my comrades showed up. This was no twerpy lunchroom competition; it was one of the year's biggest meets, and it was held in an old midtown hotel. Already there were school buses pulling up outside, disgorging teams hailing from the far reaches of the burbs.

The joint was huge. As I entered, I could see signs of decaying elegance everywhere, especially in the formerly grand lobby, but it nevertheless struck me as the kind of place where you might just want to check your mattress for *chinches de cama* before turning in. Apart from the slight seediness, it was a chess paradise. The common areas echoed with the low roar of a few hundred chess-mad kids high on adrenalin and hormones. The Village chess shops had set up tables overflowing with books and flash sets. A couple of local grandmasters were floating around, signing autographs while hawking private lessons and self-branded training software. All that chess swag flashed me back to being a little kid in Macy's at Christmastime, yearning for action figures and gaming consoles that we probably couldn't afford. I wished I could buy something, anything, just to recapture that new-toy buzz, but I didn't have the cash and anyway I didn't need any of this stuff. What was I going to do with a Smurfs chess set?

I checked out the ballroom. They weren't letting anyone in yet, but I was able to sneak a peek through a crack between doors. I caught my breath as I took in the cavernous space. This wasn't one of those slick corporate environments built for PowerPoints and rubber chicken; it was an old-fashioned, regal dance palace with gilt moldings and fading murals of chubby winged midgets. It was impressive as hell; looked like the set-up in one of those old black-and-white photos of legendary tournaments, the kind where everybody's wearing bad suits and smoking like a chimney. Had to be a couple of hundred boards laid out, each with its own electronic clock and a numbered placard so contestants could find their assigned positions. Like any chessplayer, I found a special kind of beauty in the repeating patterns of squares and pieces. It wasn't only that the geometrical array was dazzling to the eye; it was also that I could sense power and movement waiting to be unleashed. Every set-up contained within itself a game; every game held virtually infinite possibilities; every possibility meant joy or despair to some New York City kid with dreams of glory.

With an effort I broke off the reverie and dipped back to the common areas, hoping to appropriate some kind of home base for the team. There wasn't a lot of practice space available. As I roamed the halls I noticed a sign outside one of the corporate meeting rooms: "Reserved for Galton Prep." This chapped my ass. They'd actually paid for a practice room; nothing was too good for the swaggering Fraternity of Future Fatcats. Muttering curses, I rambled through the halls until I managed to locate an alcove with a small table and a few chairs. It was cramped but at least it was relatively quiet; we'd have to make do. Laid out my stuff to stake a claim; texted everyone to let them know where I was. While I waited for my teammates I checked out the passing players. I was amused to see that lot of them were sporting matching tees and polos. Our geeky gesture of solidarity in Sunnyside hadn't gone unnoticed.

Esther and Maggie showed up arm-in-arm as usual; Zamir followed a few minutes later. He was ordinarily an early bird type but he was still learning the intricacies of the subway system. By now the place was filling up with players from every corner of the city. The hectic scene would have been exhilarating but it was hard to ignore the draggy weirdness of playing without P.D. I felt I had to say something.

"I don't really want to give a pep talk, mostly because Zamir will call me a douche again. And I'm not going to pretend we aren't all bummed by what they did to our boy. But I'm thinking we'd do better to be pissed off than depressed. Everyone is free to handle it in their own way, but I intend to get mad, stay mad, and use my anger as motivation. I want to kick some ass for P.D."

As it turned out, my little speech was well received. Every one of us was resentful as hell and we could all get behind the idea of playing on P.D.'s behalf. We were the Furious Five and it was showtime. Zamir trotted off to the scorer's table and returned with the pairings. Maggie got matched with a mediocrity from Bayside; I drew a nerd girl from Townsend Harris, a first-rate public located in the schnazz part of Flushing. Esther checked out her opponent and broke out an evil-looking grin.

"Well, whaddya know. I'm matched with Galton's token Black kid. And get this, Mose: He's actually sporting a cashmere vee-neck sweater. He's probably wearing argyle dress socks under his kicks. I do believe I am going to have some fun with this young man."

She whipped out a bandana and wrapped up her head in an improvised doo-rag. Then she threw on her hoodie, crossed her arms tightly, and rearranged her features into a hard Brooklynesque street stare. The transformation was astonishing. She looked like a juvenile drug runner from some hackneyed exploitation movie.

"You see? I've ghetto-ized myself. I intend to project a keeping-it-real vibe, even though I'm totally faking it."

I snickered in appreciation. "You think that's going to intimidate him?"

"That, or he'll be so contemptuous of me that he'll underestimate my game. Either way, the advantage is mine. I intend to exploit his inflated ego. Vanity working on a weak head produces every sort of mischief," she Austened.

"Well, don't scare him *too* bad; he might give the cops an emergency Karen call."

"I have to admit I almost feel sorry for him. I know kids like that from the classical music scene. They're the children of professionals, under huge pressure to get into an Ivy and join the ruling class. They grow up in Caucasian spaces where they never feel they deserve to belong. The white kids love them up so they can congratulate themselves on having a Black bestie. They're never comfortable; there's always something to prove. Brutha Vee-neck probably has a crippling case of impostor syndrome."

Weirdly, I found myself feeling just a tiny bit jealous. Had I really reached that ludicrous state of insecurity in which men get salty just because shawtie says something borderline positive about another guy? Esther and I didn't even have a relationship and I was already going *Eyes Wide Shut*, just because I fancied her. The root of the problem, I realized, wasn't Esther — it was the undeniable reality that this dude had everything I didn't: money, status, first-class education, a pipeline to the Ivies.

"Well, I'm not shedding any tears for that dude. Kids like him grow up to be straw bosses; they end up getting paid to manage other Black people with less status. Like my dad says, the big corporations hire them to act as Negro wranglers. Pardon my French." (Dad, of course, hated the word "Negro"; he used it with ironic contempt to suggest, as he so often did, that corporate diversity programs are typically just a screen for old-style racism.)

"Needless to say, ain't nobody wrangling *this* girl." She'd flipped smoothly from Britspeak to Brooklynese mid-sentence. We were all chameleons when we needed to be, but no one pulled it off with more style than Esther. Then she shot me a severe look. "And don't talk to me about French, boy. It was my first language."

Yeesh; had I put my foot in it again? Lately I really cared what Esther thought of me; it was a little disconcerting. I looked abashed; evidently that was enough for her. She gave me a shoulder punch and something close enough to a smile that I sensed I'd been granted absolution.

We broke camp and headed for our tables. Townsend Harris had rigorous selective admissions, so presumably my opponent was some kind of geek-brain, though tbh she seemed kinda sweet. Reminded me of Maggie. Opposite this nice girl, I just couldn't get motivated by rage. So I resolved instead to play like Botvinnik, unaffected by emotions, floating serenely in the 64-square universe. It worked, more or less. I played Blackmar-Diemer and she responded by the book for a few moves, but I exploited the initiative and kept her on the defensive. She bungled a complex trade in the middle game and I ended up with a one-piece advantage. She sighed and resigned. Her capitulation was probably premature but I wasn't complaining. I could tamp down my rage and still find a way to win one for the Gipper.

Afterwards I spotted Zamir on the other side of the ballroom and flagged him down. We retreated to a corner and quietly discussed our games. He'd drawn one of the better players from Bronx Science, not a superstar but definitely on the high end of scholastic chess. Zamir had to take him all the way to the endgame; pressed a pawn advantage and made his point. We were about to beat it back to our alcove when we heard a sudden explosive bang. I flinched and a hundred heads swiveled toward the big double doors as a darkly-clad figure swept into the hall, trailing a cloud of blue razz vapor. A black duster raincoat swirled around his ankles as he skated towards the pairings board. Gimlet-eyed and poised for action, he looked like a Mexican gunslinger in a spaghetti Western — like the great Volonté in fact. It was, of course, P.D., hurried and grimly determined but working his dramatic flair to the max.

Immobilized with astonishment, we watched as he strode between the rows of tables and located his board, where a sleepy-eyed kid from Yeshiva suddenly jerked to attention. He'd been assigned white; when P.D. failed to show he just played e4 and started the clock. He'd been reading *Harry Potter* as the time ran down, counting on the forfeit and assuming he had the win in the bag. Then P.D. swooped down on him like some kind of predatory bird. He advanced a pawn and slapped the clock even before he sat down. He couldn't have had more than five minutes left on the clock and couldn't afford to get sucked into a complex endgame. He'd need to use blitz tactics to force a quick, decisive win.

We couldn't see the position from our corner but we could read the body language. P.D. was snapping down pieces with machine-like efficiency. About two minutes into the game we could see his opponent suddenly deflate like a blown retread. Evidently P.D. had pulled off something masterly. He snatched the white queen from the board and the Yeshiva kid froze. He stared at the position for five minutes and tentatively advanced a piece. P.D responded instantly; he was raining death on the poor kid. After a couple more moves they shook hands. Had to be checkmate.

We intercepted P.D. on his way out of the ballroom. Zamir grabbed him and pounded his back, laughing; I gave him a vigorous bump and steered him toward our alcove. Esther and Maggie were already in place — they'd both won their games — and they actually squealed like Middle School fangirls when P.D. materialized.

"What the hell happened, meegs?" I asked. "We had you marked down as perma-dead."

"Ever heard of a *deus ex machina*?"

"Heard of it; not quite sure what it means."

"Listen and learn, grasshopper. We had this last semester in World Lit. Literally it means 'god from the machine.' It's a narrative cheat. Whenever those ancient Greek playwrights maneuvered their characters into an impossible situation, they'd roll in a crane and lower some dude in a God costume down to the stage. Waves a wand; settles the beefs. Audience goes home happy. You see this kind of scam all the time in cheesy cable shows — you know, when the writer can't figure out a way to dig himself out of a plot hole. SWAT team rides in at the last minute, guns blazing."

"Sure, they do the same thing in, like, every single Hercules flick ever made."

"Exactly. It's a relief to know I can always rely on your shitty taste in movies to assist you in comprehending reality. So anyway, last night I'm staring at my phone, brooding about how I'm irrevocably screwed. *Ping!* Email from Doctor Evil. I open it up, figuring it's an official notice that I'm about to get expelled or otherwise annihilated. Instead, she tells me that all my restrictions have been lifted. No explanation. She throws in some boilerplate threatening language, but it reads like the kind of face-saving bullshit you can safely ignore."

I snorted with laughter. "Can't help it; I'm picturing Sanprudencio's big old boody swinging over the stage on a crane. An image that will haunt my nightmares."

"Verily, my lad. But what has been thought cannot be unthought. You must now live with the *gluteus ex machina*."

"So you're in the clear?"

"Looks that way. She had the gall to add some corporate-sounding happy talk, basically advising me that I'm supposed to bring honor to the school and my own sad self by winning buttloads of chess games. Upshot is, I've been expunged from the Bad Boy Book and loosed from the leash."

Esther gave me a curious glance. "Why do I have the feeling that you were behind this, Middleton? No secrets among comrades: Lay it on us."

"I'm as surprised as you are. For now let's say I may have been peripherally involved, but I don't know the backstory. As soon as I find out I'll give everyone the full S.P. Meanwhile, tell us what transpired with your Double Stuf from Galton."

"Psyched him out. When we met I hosed him down with all kinds of ghetto hostility. Then, when he played the French, I shot him the scornful variation of the Death Stare — the one that says "*Really*?" She demonstrated with an ultra-withering glare. "I locked eyes with him, crossed my arms, and sat there, perfectly still, for maybe a full minute till his confidence crashed and he looked away. From that moment I *owned* the muffa."

"Nice work, milady."

"That wasn't even the best part. After he resigned, I thanked him for the game with outrageously high-toned politesse. He couldn't reconcile the Britspeak with the doo-rag. He looked ready to implode. Bad case of cognitive dissonance."

Maggie had won, too, I was happy to learn. As we played through her game I was struck by how aggressive and confident she'd become over the board, and I hoped it would carry over into real life. She was no longer the timid, vulnerable creature I'd known since Middle School; she was evolving into something formidable. It was as though she was channeling our team solidarity into a newfound emotional strength. The Viktor Effect.

Our first round had been everything we could have hoped for, in spite of the lofty level of competition. We had P.D. back in harness, we were perfect so far, and — perhaps more importantly given our central goal — we'd already stolen a point from the Galtonians. We were fulfilling the promise of our off-the-cob tees.

Now, of course, we'd all be facing winners. This time I drew a Galton kid, so the pressure was on me. Somehow I wasn't surprised to discover that it was my nemesis, the same callow clown who'd psyched me out with Scholar's Mate at 722's tournament. It had been just a few weeks ago but it seemed like a lifetime. No French Defense for me this time; I had a hunch that Young Massa would run Scholar's again. I was right, and this time I kept my head (thanks, Comrade Pushkin) and punished him. Deploying both knights, I chased his queen all the way back to d1. Got my queen's bishop out and monstered him. A couple of moves later he was faced with a choice between mate and a lost queen. He resigned, offering his flaccid (*vocab!*) pink hand. *Déjà vu* — only this time it was Paleface being forced to acknowledge his new boss. Gratifying to say the least. Another point for us; one less for Galton.

Back at the ranch, I learned that Maggie, Esther, and P.D. had all won. To everyone's shock, however, Zamir had been bested by one of the strongest players in the tournament, a kid from Stuyvesant with a master-level Elo. In the long run, I was sure, Zamir would have the juice to compete with dudes like that, but he was still a relative novice and not quite prepared for the meat grinder you experience at the highest levels of play. Zamir wasn't crushed on a personal level — his disposition was too sunny for that — but he felt bad about letting us down and apologized to each of us so profusely that it was a little embarrassing. Maggie stepped in and sweetly smoothed things over. Gave him a little smooch on the cheek and ruffled his hair. I was glad to see it, though if I'd still been crushing on her I might have been a little jelly.

"Zamir, you are my Albanian Naruto," she said. "I have faith in you always. The hero will return to fight and triumph again."

I'm pretty sure Zamir didn't even know who Naruto was, but it didn't matter. He felt the warmth and immediately recovered his usual exuberance.

Third Round. I'm black against some smartass from Adam Clayton Powell. He made a slighting remark about my T-shirt as he started his clock. Wasn't impressed; didn't care. I just let it go and focused on the game. He played Queen's Gambit. I was more than ready; I knew this opening inside and out. Ran the Albin countergambit, a risky, super-aggressive response, and I could tell right away he hadn't seen it before. He blundered into the Lasker trap and the whole thing was in my pocket after nine moves. Worked him.

There was a scheduled lunch break before the final round so we had a chance to take stock. We met downstairs in the hotel sandwich shop. Over a big greasy spread of deluxe cheeseburgers, Zamir shared what he'd learned about the state of the tournament. Stuy, Powell, and Bronx Science were kicking ass as expected; their top four players were all 3-0. No chance of winning of course, but it was nevertheless a miraculous showing for 722. A month or two ago we'd been at best a mediocrity among Queens publics; now we were more than holding our own in the city's biggest, strongest tournament.

But what of the class enemy? We appeared to be just about even with Galton, floating around seventh or eighth place. P.D., Maggie and I all had three wins, while Zamir and Esther had two apiece. Gang Galton was a similar position; three players had three points apiece. Zamir's assessment of the situation was unnerving.

"I believe P.D. will win his game. Esther and I have a very good chance of finishing strong, since we will be matched against opponents with two wins. However, if we want to be assured of finishing ahead of Galton, I think that one of you two — he nodded at Maggie and me — must win this round."

Scary. Maggie and I, both perfect through three, would likely be facing Elo monsters in our final matches.

P.D., slumped in the corner of the vinyl banquette, chuckled drily.

"So now you're taking my superpowers for granted? I suppose that's the fate of the preternaturally gifted. If I win, everybody shrugs and hands me a cookie. If I lose, it's the end of the world."

"You speak truly, O godlike potentate of the chessboard," I replied. "Beasting is expected from you, every single time. Cookies optional."

I had a brief spell of optimism, but the pairings confirmed my worst fears. I was matched with one of the superstars. After lunch I trudged reluctantly toward the ballroom, hands in pockets, down in the mouth. On the way I ran into Viktor, who was presumably on his way to sneak a smoke: I could see him caressing his cigarette case. I thought I'd try to solicit some words of wisdom from our own Mister Miyagi; couldn't hurt. I explained the situation.

"Certainly the odds of winning are not good," he conceded. "But one must have hope, always. I have friends at Travers Park whose circumstances are as straitened as my own. Every month when our support checks arrive, we each buy a lottery ticket. By so doing we are making a tiny investment in hope. You know the game: If you gamble a dollar, you are purchasing an infinitesimal chance of winning the jackpot. However, if you do *not* buy the ticket, you have no chance at all. Hence the famous slogan used to promote the lottery: 'You gotta be in it to win it.' It is perhaps what you call a come-on, but it is quite literally true."

"But this isn't a matter of luck, right? Chess is all about the skills, and this guy has like 400 Elo points on me."

"My young friend, Elo is merely a tool; it is not destiny. Not long ago a 10-year old boy from Bengal defeated the grandmaster Adam Tukhaev in tournament play. The boy's rating was approximately the same as yours is now. There are many similar stories. Remember, the chess board is a site of infinite possibilities. Play this young man as you would any strong player. Refuse to be intimidated. And do please relax: Losing to him would be no shame; winning would be a small but very gratifying gift from the inscrutable gods of chess."

I shrugged; we said our good-byes; I headed for the tables. Could I beat this dude? Stranger things have happened, I supposed. I remembered my man Hercules. One of his labors was almost literally impossible. He was commanded to clean the stables of King Augeas in a single day; the king owned 30,000 head of cattle and had allowed mad mountains of cow dung to accumulate over 30 years. The Hercmeister was in no mood to shovel shit, so instead he dug trenches to divert the course of a nearby stream. In an hour the stables were washed kitchen-clean. Obviously, I wouldn't be getting any help from local natural features when I played this kid, but the point was, Hercules didn't give up when faced with an apparently insurmountable obstacle. He stayed on point, kept moving. He didn't fold, like I had back when I'd blown my chance to take the high school exams. Win or lose, I was going to bring my best to this match. No regrets.

My opponent was a rangy East Asian kid, probably a senior, who looked a little bored with the proceedings. No doubt he'd checked my rating and figured he had this one in the bag. But he was probably irritated, too, because my relatively low Elo meant he had little chance of winning the tournament. They'd be using an algorithm to pick an overall winner from the players who ended up with perfect 4-0 scores; the formula rewarded the players who had faced the strongest opposition. Beating lowly Moses Middleton wouldn't do much for his chances.

Just for the hell of it, I ran the Danish. He rolled his eyes, revealing his contempt for my inferior Elo, and accepted. He snapped his pieces down briskly and distractedly, projecting indifference and boredom. I placed my queen on e2, just to see if I could give him some headaches by vectoring the king file. Then, to my astonishment, he advanced his king's bishop pawn two squares. I stared at the board, blinking. Was this a trap? I thought I had to be missing something, but shrugged internally and forged ahead. Took his pawn, revealing check. He could've recovered by defending with his queen, forcing a trade. Instead he blocked the check with a knight, and suddenly his ass was mine. Advanced my pawn to f6. Pawn takes pawn, bishop takes pawn. Now came a colossal blunder. He positioned his queen on d7, probably thinking he could mount some sort of counterattack but forgetting that his rook was *en prise*. Grabbed his rook with my bishop and it was all over. Eleven moves. Thirty seconds off his clock. Stunning debacle for a player at his level. Evidently the gods of chess were on my side today.

Checked in with my teammates; received general plaudits and a complex ghetto-style dap from Zamir, who had won his game. The boy was learning fast. Esther won — she was beaming; she knew she was improving rapidly and digging it. Maggie lost to some superstar from Powell, but she wasn't unduly fazed since I'd stolen us a point. P.D. celebrated his return from scholastic Siberia with a crushing win over a high-powered kid from Brooklyn. So our top four players had amassed 14 points. Would it be enough to put Galton down? Nerding out unashamedly, I flipped open my laptop and repeatedly refreshed the tournament results page, waiting for the team totals. Suspense? It was Hitchcockian.

18. RED SALUTE

After what seemed like a thousand hard refreshes, the display flickered and the final tallies rolled in. Well, blow me sideways: We'd done it. Just barely. Good old 722, the acme of so-so, ended up in a three-way tie for fifth place; Galton, nipping at our reinforced sneaker heels, finished sixth. Mission accomplished: a moral victory like no other. Bronx Science, a dark horse, won the tournament, but we barely noticed. We were screaming, jumping up and down, cheering like maniacs. I even started a chant: "We're Number Five! We're Number Five!" Got some funny looks from the other teams but I had no effs to give. In your face, Galton — in your pale, exquisitely groomed face.

In the middle of all this I noticed that P.D. was staring at me with a look of ironic amusement.

"Yo, Hercules: I hate to interrupt your celebration of mediocrity, but you're four and O. That means you're in the running for the individual championship.

It actually hadn't occurred to me, but I played it cool.

"Doubtless, my brother — and pigs might fly. Hogs might hover. The Mets might win the pennant."

The tournament organizers would be running their unfathomable algorithm behind the scenes and keeping the results on the downlow till they could announce the winner at the closing ceremony. I didn't give it much thought, simply assuming I'd be an also-ran as usual. I'd momentarily forgotten the essential issue: The computer program took account of the relative strengths of the players, awarding extra points for vanquishing opponents with higher ratings. So my mediocrity could work to my advantage, especially since I'd (almost accidentally) defeated a guy with a master-level Elo.

Weirdly, wonderfully, that's exactly what happened. Everyone gathered in the ballroom to hear the results and collect their tchotchkes. I was deep in a whispered conversation with P.D., who was fervently recommending a *giallo* horror movie that featured piquant forms of mutilation, when my name was called. I didn't even hear it. Esther grabbed my shoulder and shook me.

"Snap to attention, Moses. You won the damn thing."

I knew I didn't deserve it. I wasn't the strongest player there by a long way — on a good day, I'd be lucky to make the top 50 — and I was probably already scraping the ceiling of my chess skills. I'd never be as good as Zamir or P.D. I'd lucked out and beat the algorithm through an unrepeatable event. Made me feel like a fraud. I feared I was about to contract a devastating case of impostor syndrome, just like Brutha Vee-neck.

But what the hell. When Hercules cleaned the Augean stables with hydropower, that was kind of a cheat too. King Eurystheus — the Sanprudencio of ancient Argos — certainly thought so. He figured Herc had pulled a Lance Armstrong; made him do another labor to compensate. But Herc prevailed, and if it was good enough for my Hellenic hero, it was good enough for me. Score one for Moses Middleton.

I mounted the ballroom's bandstand in a daze. The emcee handed me a heavy, gingerbready trophy that resembled the spaceship from Close Encounters. It was — to use a word that might actually appear on the SATs — *rococo.* I posed for a pic with the tournament director; felt like I was photobombing my own self. Scanned the crowd. I saw my high-powered Stuyvesant opponent scowling. I spotted my surfer buddy Lee flashing me a thumbs-up. Way in the back, I saw Viktor smiling broadly, his nicotine-stained teeth visible all the way across the room. And then I saw my teammates, easily identifiable by their matching, defiantly nerdy red shirts, shoulder to shoulder, obviously elated. Slowly P.D. raised his fist. One by one, my teammates did the same. A magnificent red salute. I tried to capture a mental image: This was a moment I intended to remember all my life.

* * *

Lugging my tatty trophy homeward with a mixture of pride and embarrassment, I ran into Mallika on the stoop. She made noises of admiration, and I responded as politely as I could, but I wanted to change the subject. I was desperate to find out what she'd done to raise P.D. from the tomb.

"You must be magic!" I blurted. "What kind of miracle did you work?"

It was all I could do to keep from giving her a jubilant chest bump — not something she was likely to appreciate, no matter how well intentioned. So I restricted myself to grasping her hand and thanking her breathlessly.

"It was nothing, Mose, especially given the ammunition you supplied. Merely a little backroom lawyering. Ordinarily, you should know, I disapprove of cancel culture. Destroying people on the basis of social media posts has a chilling effect on people's willingness to communicate honestly. However, I considered myself to be acting as P.D.'s advocate, and when I advocate, I advocate *vigorously*. I informed your nemesis of what we had found and suggested an option that would allow us to keep the information confidential."

"So you aren't going to get her fired?"

"Certainly not. If I were to expose Doctor Sanprudencio publicly, the best we could hope for would be a transfer to some sort of obscure desk job pending a disciplinary proceeding. Meanwhile, she would doubtless be replaced by someone equally bad, or worse. And P.D. would remain on probation indefinitely. I felt that the best outcome would be to turn the tables on her, to make her accountable to the kids under her care. So we came to an informal agreement. She promised to call off the dogs; in return, I agreed to take no action so long as I was satisfied that P.D. was not being harassed or persecuted. She'll remain in office but she'll need to keep me — and the members of the chess club — very happy indeed going forward. As they say in *The Godfather*: 'Keep your friends close and your enemies closer.'"

"I see your point. But what about the rest of the school? She's a power-mad racist and she's bound to make trouble for other kids."

"We discussed that, implicitly. I suggested to her that she could easily be deemed unfit to work with a student body as diverse as 722's. And I informed her that, should I become aware of incidents reflecting racist or anti-immigrant attitudes on her part, I would be ethically obligated to take further action. I think your classmates will find her much more, shall we say, *accommodating* in future."

"Whoa, I'm impressed. That is one evil scheme. Forgive me — you know I mean that in the nicest way."

"No worries, Moses, I know exactly what you mean. But consider this: Maybe, in the long run, this will be good for Dr. Sanprudencio. If she spends the next few semesters giving meaningful assistance to students — or, at the very least, refraining from thwarting them — she just might discover that right behavior has its rewards. Perhaps she'll earn a little respect and find that she enjoys it. Maybe students will actually begin to *like* her and she'll bask in the warmth. Hard as it may be to believe, people can change, especially when they're given a solid nudge in the right direction. Given time, Doctor Evil could become Doctor Love."

I couldn't see it, but I figured I'd give Mallika the benefit of the doubt. I'd never met someone simultaneously so tough and so wise, with the possible exception of Viktor. We strolled through the door, arm in arm.

Most of the housemates were inside, and of course I couldn't get around showing off that big ugly trophy, even though I felt like a phony. Lavish congratulations all round; it was pretty excruciating. I tried to explain that I'd stolen the win, and so a repeat performance wasn't on the menu, but they were having none of it. Mom squealed and gave me the hug to end all hugs; Dad shook my hand and said something 'inspirational' about how this was only the first of many triumphs to come. The first of many labors, I thought to myself: Like Hercules, I knew I was going to have to bust it, repeatedly, to earn my props. The trophy was given a place of honor in the living room adjacent to my parents' favorite adorable photos of yours truly, compounding the embarrassment. So this was victory: a tacky plastic loving cup and accolades from people who'd praise you no matter what you did. Seriously, though, I was proud: When my teammates needed me, I'd had their back. It had taken all of us together to defeat the class enemy.

* * *

The next morning I got a disturbing phone call from Esther. No accents or Austening; she spoke rapidly and forcefully.

"Maggie called me. Things have gone critical at her house. That disgusting pervert finally crossed the line. Maggie was so upset she was incoherent, so it was hard to tell exactly what happened, but evidently he fondled Maggie's butt last night and her mom saw it. She went ballistic and ordered him out of the house. He has to vacate before sundown."

"Does Maggie think he's going to leave?"

"She can't say for sure. He got drunk and started weeping, putting on a big show of being victimized and suicidal. Then he threatened to report Maggie's mom to Child Protective Services. She told him 'fine, do your worst,' or words to that effect. She gave him all the cash in the house and said she never wanted to see him again. I guess now that she's landed a respectable job, her confidence is back and she's not going to take any more shit from him."

"Does Maggie feel safe?"

"She's scared. She's alone with him right now. Locked herself in her room."

"Here's an idea: I think she needs to come over and stay at my place until everything chills out. She'll have plenty of protection over here."

"I was hoping you'd say that."

"Give me a few minutes to explain the situation to my parents. Tell Maggie I'm on my way over and I'll text her as soon as I get there. She can throw together an overnight bag if she wants, but we've probably got everything she needs for a short stay. I'll walk her back to my place."

Found Mom in the kitchen and explained the situation; she responded as expected.

"Bring her right over. She can stay as long as she needs to. Mrs. Wang too. It has fallen upon you, mortal, to do great deeds."

"I am honored, O venerable enchantress."

I hit the street and booked off toward Maggie's place. I was sweatin' but it felt good to actually be *doing* something about the situation.

My phone chimed as I ambled down the sidewalk; thought I'd let it go to voicemail as I usually did, but something told me to pick up. It was Maggie, sounding breathless and terrified.

"Mose, you have to help me. Chen dragged me to the subway; now he's threatening to jump in front of a train. I don't know what to do."

"Damn! Where are you?"

"82nd Street No. 7 train. Flushing side."

This was the elevated train, running high above Roosevelt Avenue, the busy dividing line between Jackson Heights and Elmhurst. I was about three blocks away. I started to run.

"I'm on my way. Did you call the cops?"

"Yes, but I don't know how long they'll take to get here."

"How far away is the train?"

I pictured her peering down the tracks, where you could see the inbound trains coming on.

"Looks like about three stops. Hurry!"

I broke the connection and sprinted up Roosevelt toward the station, dodging shoppers and churro stands like a maniacal hurdler. I figured I had three, maybe four, minutes. The sidewalk was the usual riot of activity: Mariachi music was blaring; kids were dribbling a soccer ball; I could smell roast corn and arepas. This was the authentic local color that the gentrifiers loved to sample, just so long as it was completely isolated from the Historic District a couple of blocks to the north. The street hawkers, with their cheap toys and phone cases and melon slices, were ordinarily one of my favorite things about the hood; now they were infuriating obstacles to my progress. It felt like every person and object on the street was conspiring to slow me down.

In the end, I managed to negotiate the short blocks uptown without too much trouble. But for some reason the south-side entrances were roped off. I would need to dash across Roosevelt before I could access the steps to the Flushing-bound platform. By the time I made it to the corner of 82nd Street, the traffic light was against me. Of course. I knew from vexing experience that it could take something like two minutes for that signal to change. No choice: I had to hurl myself into traffic and hope for the best.

I dived between two parked cars and emerged inches away from a passing yuppie cyclist, who swerved, nearly clipping me, and screamed some abuse (couldn't blame the guy, despite his ridiculous time trial helmet and bib-style ball-squeezers.) Horns blared; drivers shouted obscenities. I launched myself right in front of a taxi, one of those green jobs licensed for the boroughs. He stomped on his brakes and the squeal was earsplitting. He stopped in time

— just — and his front bumper made soft contact with my leg. I almost soiled my draws but kept going. Reached the sidewalk unscathed and headed for the foot of the staircase that leads up to the elevated platform. I was steaming ahead, taking the stairs two at a time, when I encountered an insurmountable obstacle. Two guys were wrestling a massive cardboard box down to the street; there was no way around them. I reversed, hit the sidewalk, and shot across 82nd to the other entrance. This time the stairs were clear. Made it to the vestibule where the turnstiles were located; pulled out my wallet and swiped my MetroCard. The tacky little electronic sign lit up: "Insufficient fare."

Un. Effing. Believable. No way I had time to top up the card. Near panic, I did what Dad had warned me never to do under any circumstances, lest I draw unwanted attention from the popo: I jumped the turnstile. Didn't even pause to check for cops. For once I was in luck: No one stopped me or called me out. I charged up the second set of stairs to the platform, feeling like a prize dick as I shouldered aside a couple of slow-moving citizens, who scolded me in stark terms. Reached the top at last. Gasping for breath, I leaned out over the track and glanced toward Manhattan. The Flushing-bound train had already pulled out of 74th Street; it would be here inside of a minute.

The station was mobbed as always. I scanned left and right, desperately trying to pick Maggie and Chen out of the crowd. Spotted them at the extreme west end of the platform. Chen was standing right at the edge; Maggie was hanging on to his shirtsleeve, apparently trying to pull him back from the precipice. Once again I sprinted, weaving around clumps of straphangers. Made it with a few seconds to spare. Grabbed him in a bearhug as the train rolled in, brakes screeching.

To my surprise he didn't struggle at all but allowed me to manhandle him, pretty gently, away from the tracks. We ended up against the platform wall, face to face with my hands steadying his shoulders. Maggie looked on from a safe distance as I tried, gasping, to talk him down unthreateningly, the way they always do on the cop shows.

"Let's be really cool now, okay?"

"Okay, okay. Everything fine," he said.

He looked me straight in the eye and I saw something hard and calculating in his gaze. I detected, too, just a hint of a contemptuous sneer on his lips. I realized instantly that this was not a desperate man on the brink of suicide; this was the same old Chen, fully in control and calculating, getting ready to manipulate the situation to his advantage. I lost it.

"Why you unspeakable drama queen, you had absolutely no intention of offing yourself. This whole scene was a hoax, just a ploy to hold onto your meal ticket. That's why you let Maggie call me. That's why you didn't put up any kind of a fight."

I let go of his shoulders and stepped back. I was furious, but I caught my breath and tried to speak calmly. I wanted to emulate P.D., remembering how his air of quiet menace was far more intimidating than the kind of confrontational screaming you hear every day on the street.

"Listen, dickhead, you just played your last card. You've got maybe two minutes to get out of here before the cops show up. Go back to the house, grab whatever stuff you can carry with you and then GTFO. Disappear. Melt into the crowd. I don't care what the hell you do. Just vanish. Or I'm going to call La Migra, the police, and every city office I can think of, just to get you locked in a cage. I've never snitched on anybody in my life, but in your case I'll gladly make an exception."

He looked at me with obvious hatred and hissed some words at me; it was mostly unintelligible but definitely culminated with the N-word. He was trying to provoke me. I refused to play.

"Here's what's going to happen. I'm taking Maggie home with me now. I'm coming back to her place tonight with plenty of backup. When we get there, you'd better be long gone. Otherwise, one way or another, I'm going to see you in Riker's. Tell me you understand." I shook him gently. "Tell me."

All of a sudden the ferocious light in his eyes dimmed and I could feel his muscles relax into passivity. He'd given up. It was over.

"Yeah, okay, I understand." He broke away from me, turned on his heels, and speed-walked across the platform and down the stairs. Screw him, anyhow: It was time to think about Maggie.

She was shaking. I put an arm around her and tried to be reassuring.

"This is all going to work out, I promise you. We have some high-powered, pissed-off adults on the case."

I steered her back to my house, where my mom welcomed her with a warm embrace. She was going to be smothered with affectionate support, the way I used to be when I was a kid and came home with a skinned knee or a bad scare. We set her up in Allegra's room, which had an extra bed. Allegra was happy to share some basic overnight stuff — pajamas, cosmetics, various mysterious things that women seem to need wherever they go. Dad rustled up a spare toothbrush while Mom guided Maggie downstairs to the kitchen, where she immediately set about fixing sandwiches. In my mother's family tradition, there was no such thing as a predicament that couldn't be improved with generous helpings of food. It's a wonder we aren't a bunch of chonks with heart conditions.

I briefed Mallika and she got Mrs. Wang on the phone. She advised coming straight over — there was no telling what that duplicitous (*vocab!*) slimebag might do now that he was backed into a corner. Mrs. Wang showed up on our doorstep half an hour later. Chen hadn't come home yet, she said, but she was beginning to hope that this was the end. She'd gathered all his stuff and dumped it into a contractor bag; left it outside the door. We were all crossing our fingers, betting that he'd understand how serious we all were and vanish without any more drama. Everyone gathered in the living room — Julian, Ritwik, and Dante were at work, so Dad and I were the only men present — and what followed was probably the most spectacular group cry to take place in northern Queens since Carlos Beltran struck out looking in Game Seven of the NLCS. The women were weeping partly from sadness, partly from vestiges of fear (the guys might also have shed a manly tear or two, though I'm keeping that information on a need-to-know basis). But I think it was mostly relief: It now seemed certain that the *mishegas* was nearing some kind of resolution.

We made a plan. After giving Chen time to vacate, we were simply going to stroll over to Maggie's place *en masse*, seeking safety — and power — in numbers. My dad would call a locksmith to meet us there; seemed like a good idea to change the locks on the spot. I knew Esther would never forgive me if she wasn't a part of this, so I texted her the essentials; she cut her fencing lesson and headed over. At this point it seemed stupid not to inform the rest of the team. Maggie was okay with it. So I got P.D. and Zamir on the phone and explained; they, too, dropped everything and vectored toward the stately Middleton residence.

Knowing Mom would spot me a little extra caffeine under these trying circumstances, I brewed up an immense pot of coffee. As the whole gang trickled in there was time to pour everybody a fortifying cup.

It was the first time P.D. had seen our place. As my parents welcomed him, he went full Eddie Haskell.

"Good afternoon, Mrs. Middleton, Mr. Middleton. Is the Beav at home?" He flashed a winning grin; P.D. was all charm when he wanted to be.

My mom laughed, made apologies for her failure to visit the hairdresser that morning, and said something about vacuuming the rugs in high heels and pearls.

Zamir, weirdly, understood the joke. (I later discovered that he'd been raised on subtitled reruns of *Leave It to Beaver.*)

"*Mirë, Wally, kjo eshte e mrekullueshme,*" he said. "This is the Albanian for 'Gee, Wally, that's swell.'"

Esther showed up wearing a puffy jacket — it was chilly that day; there had even been a couple of snow flurries — and when she took it off I could see that she was still attired in her fencing uniform; she'd dashed right over from the Queens Fencing Club in Flushing. I tried not to stare; couldn't help noticing how hot she looked in that form-fitting white jacket. Sure, we might have been dealing with a major crisis, but the adolescent hormones remained in full effect.

"Pity you couldn't bring your saber, milady. You might need to call the villain out."

"He is welcome to meet me behind the Luxembourg at one o'clock, providing he brings a long wooden box."

"*Three Musketeers*?"

"*Certainement, mon chéri.* There is no situation in life that has not been anticipated and understood by the great Dumas, who is second only to Austen in the pantheon."

"All for one and one for all, that's for sure," I said. And a more vivid embodiment of Dumas' famous phrase would be hard to imagine as we mustered in an untidy phalanx, preparing to escort Maggie and mama back to their place. Dark was falling on the tree-lined streets. It was late afternoon, and either Chen would already be long gone or we'd need to make a new plan on the fly. We threw on our coats and flowed onto the sidewalk. Mallika was way out ahead, marching briskly like she was going to war. The rest of us followed, surrounding the Wangs like a Secret Service security detail. We had the swagger; all we needed to complete the picture was matching pairs of Oakley Zeros, and maybe some of those lo-tech Fed earpieces with coiled wires attached.

What awaited us at Maggie's apartment was a welcome anticlimax. The garbage bag was gone from the stoop; the place was dark and quiet. We knocked and rang the bell a couple of times to make absolutely sure nobody was home. No response. Maggie unlocked the door and P.D. insisted on going in first, assuming a defensive crouch like a SWAT team guy on cable. He proceeded to check every room and eventually waved us in. All clear. The only trace of Chen was a Chinese graffito scrawled by fingertip on the bathroom mirror; Maggie said it meant something nasty and declined to translate.

So it looked like the Pervy Uncle show was cancelled at last. Maybe he was on the streets; maybe he was checking into one of those roach motels in Chinatown or Flushing; maybe he was finding his way back to China. None of us gave a good goddamn. The relief was palpable. The locksmith showed up in his van, and while he did his thing Mrs. Wang and Allegra quietly discussed her immediate plans. She said she felt safe to stay in the apartment; no need for a sleepover. Maggie agreed, with an uncharacteristic display of joyous enthusiasm.

"This place feels like home for the first time in a long time," she said. "I want to enjoy it. It is going to be so cool to be able to do my homework without worrying about being messed with. And I think I'm going to have my best sleep in months. Thank you all. *So* much."

Another mighty group hug ensued. Even P.D. briefly dropped his chill façade and joined the gang. After we disentangled ourselves, a teary-eyed Maggie turned to me and smiled.

"Mose, without you none of this good stuff would've happened."

"Nah, couldn't have done anything by myself. We *all* did this."

Then, to my surprise, Maggie wrapped her arms around me, squeezed hard, and gave me a little peck on the cheek.

"You're my legendary hero anyway," she whispered.

Cool. Maybe life in the Friend Zone wasn't so bad after all.

19. AN OPENING MOVE

On a chilly morning some weeks later I woke up in a panic. My alarm hadn't buzzed; I was screwed. Sprang out of bed muttering a colorful skein of obscenities but then, with a feeling of relief so intense it was almost worth the moment of heart-stopping dread, I realized it was Spring Break. My time was my own and I had nothing in particular to worry about.

The troubles of late winter were over, I had to figure. Somehow I'd made it through the past couple of weeks without any earthshaking crises or threatened beatdowns. Mrs. Wang was settling nicely into her new job and had already made the first payment on the loan. Maggie was happier and healthier than I'd ever seen her — no Chen, no worries. P.D. was showing up for school most days and, to his acute embarrassment, had become a special project for Doctor Evil. She showcased a short story he'd written in lit class; got him enrolled in a film studies seminar at Queens College. (I was a little perturbed: If he ended up surpassing me in deep knowledge of movie lore, he'd own me in every possible way.) Sanprudencio was constantly buttonholing him in the halls and summoning him to her office for what she called "caring sessions." He was ambivalent about all this to say the least. The amount of time he spent hanging out with her was becoming a school joke. Once I even ventured to taunt him, in what I thought was a good-natured way, by singing "Dear Prudence" — until he threatened to go Krav Maga on my ass.

Esther — well, Esther had her own things, the music and the fencing, and I wasn't seeing much of her outside of chess club. We were keeping up with the weekly social gatherings that Viktor had prescribed, taking in a couple of movies and a few diner dinners, but I felt like I wasn't really connecting with Esther. Sometimes I worried that she was ignoring me, that I'd said or done something that had shut down any potential for getting closer. I was so leery of screwing it up that I did nothing at all, reverting to the meek mild Moses of old. *Ha osato tutto?* Not where cute girls are concerned. Maybe I could brave fists and fire and brutal punishments, but the possibility of humiliation still stopped me cold.

I had a meet-up with Zamir that morning. We were going to swing by Travers Park, see if we could find Viktor and grab a couple of games. Picked him up outside of his apartment building, looking forward to an awkward new T-shirt. But he surprised me. He was sporting the yellow-on-black classic Wutang shirt, along with a smart new pair of street-ready kicks. My boy was evolving fast, well on the way to becoming cool, and I have to admit I felt a little wistful. I was going to miss my Albanian power nerd.

"You're looking mad Brummel today, my lad. Where'd you get the tee?"

"It is a gift from P.D. He dug it out of his closet. He said he was taking charge of my look from now on."

"A wiser fashion adviser you could not find. Shall we skittle?"

We found Viktor at his usual table, puffing away and studying a massive Russian-language chess book.

"It is Lipnitsky's *Questions of Modern Chess Theory*," he explained. "It was considered essential when I was a young man. It has not been translated into English. Perhaps the two of you should consider learning the Russian language. You will find that a scandalous number of important books from the Soviet era are unavailable in English, including my own if I may say so. Your rulers would prefer to erase the history and culture of our noble experiment — one that continues to embarrass them, decades after it was crushed."

Viktor was on Commie overdrive that day, which I liked, for his sake. In this mood he was full of energy and purpose, and it was a joy to be around him. "I don't know if I could handle Russian and Italian at the same time," I admitted.

"Then allow me to recommend an Italian theoretician whom you might find interesting. Palmiro Togliatti. He was a strong amateur chess player as well as a founder of the Italian Communist Party. We named a city after him. You might find that his lectures on fascism are as relevant to the present day as they were in the 1930s. Alternatively, you might wish to investigate his comrade Antonio Gramsci, one of the most important thinkers of the 20th Century."

Whoa. Sometimes Viktor expected too much of us. I guess it was flattering that he assumed I was eager to take on Marxist scholarship in the original Italian, but to be honest I was having problems enough mastering pre-calc. And though I was intrigued and sometimes inspired by Viktor's worldview, I wasn't quite ready to dive into the deep end. I sure couldn't see myself as one of those earnest young sectarians hawking papers on the corner. Even my Red grandparents suspected that Viktor's memories of the Soviet Union were colored by nostalgia and wishful thinking. Still, nothing had ever given me more satisfaction than joining forces with my comrades to slap a toe-tag on the class enemy — and if that was communism, I was down.

Anyhow, I added two more names to the endless reading list in my head, wondering whether a lifetime was long enough for all the stuff I felt I should absorb. Maybe I could wait for the sword-and-sandals movie version: *Ercole contro i fascisti.*

"Where did you get the book, Mr. Fleischmann?" Zamir asked. "I thought you had to leave everything behind when you left the Soviet Union."

"As luck would have it, I managed to connect with a small circle of old comrades at the citywide tournament. One of them lent me the book. We now meet regularly. It is a balm for our troubled souls."

So Viktor, too, was in a much better place than he'd been just a few weeks ago. Happy days all round for Grandmaster Fleisch and the Furious Five. Viktor gave us a few games, crushing me smartly but treating Zamir with a modicum of respect. In the middle of one of their games he actually had to pause and think for a few seconds before making his move.

"I am pleased with both of you," he announced, snapping his cigarette case closed and rising from the table. "Especially you, Zamir: I believe you have the makings of a true chess player. You will excuse me now please. I am on my way to a West Village chess shop to test the declining skills of my old friends, who are as decrepit as I am."

Before we parted, I gave him a little token of appreciation. I had ordered another Furious Five T-shirt, size XL.

"I don't expect you to wear it, but I hope you'll keep it as a memento."

Viktor smiled wolfishly. "My deepest thanks. I certainly *will* wear this extraordinary garment — but not in public."

Zamir and I crossed the park, heading west toward our neighborhoods, talking music and movies. An unpleasant surprise awaited us. As fate would have it — and, to judge by the events of the past few weeks, fate would have it any way it damn well pleased with Moses Middleton — we ran straight into Marco and Steve, who were propping up the outdoor handball structure and trying to act hard. Here, looking me straight in the face with the vacant stare of the hopeless dumbass, was the payback I'd been dreading for weeks. Marco leered.

"Well, whaddya know," he said, unfolding his arms and stepping in our direction. "It's 722's cutest couple. I promised I was gonna jump you. And I never break a promise."

He scanned the playground theatrically. "Oh goodness gracious me, little girls! I've looked everywhere but I don't see your daddy P.D. You got nobody to run and cry to. C'mon, Steve, let's light up their sorry asses."

I glanced ruefully at Zamir. We were toast — *burnt* toast. Or so I thought. To my astonishment, Steve stepped into Marco's path, laid a hand on his shoulder, and spoke to him quietly.

"Dude, lay off. These guys are okay. Just leave them alone."

Marco swiveled toward his henchman in evident shock.

"Whoa. Who puffed sand up your ass?"

"Nobody, man. I'm cool."

"So just what the hell are you thinking?"

Steve drew a deep breath and came out with the longest speech I'd ever known him to deliver.

"If you really wanna know, here's the thing: Me and you have been hanging out since Middle School. It's been kinda fun, I guess. But I never, like, *got* anything from being your buddy. Right now Zamir is teaching me to freestyle like he can do. It's awesome. He's my friend now. And any friend of his is cool with me."

Light dawned. So *this* was the guerilla strategy Zamir had been hinting at. Instead of taking on the evil twins directly, he'd found a point of weakness and zeroed in. He'd recruited Steve with spectacular soccer tricks, and Marco was suddenly isolated.

"WTF, man," Marco exclaimed. His bravado was slipping away; a whine crept into his voice. "You think you're gonna trade me in for these little panty riders? You wanna be a faggot, just like them?"

Steve shrugged and made a half-hearted appeal.

"Ain't no reason I can't be friends with you and them at the same time."

Marco scowled and sputtered. "Well, actually, yeah. Yeah, there is, 'cause — ." Long pause. Then he burst out yelling, furiously. "'Cause I'm *done* with you, you pussy-ass muffa!"

He was flushed, wild-eyed, sweating. He made a tentative move toward Steve, like he intended to throw down, but quickly thought better of it. He was the kind of bully who needed back-up to feel tough; he'd never dare to take on anybody one-on-one. Steve, for his part, was unmoved. Showing Marco his back, he turned to Zamir and asked whether he had time for a lesson.

A couple of beats passed in silence. Then Marco just wilted. His face collapsed and for one dreadful moment I was afraid he was going to burst into tears. Instead, he wheeled around and jogged out of the park. He was so thoroughly deflated he didn't even bother to toss the bird. Zamir's cunning strategy had worked brilliantly. I had a strong feeling that we weren't going to have any more trouble from our Mister G wannabe — not, at least, until he managed to find some fresh drooling dickwit to carry his gym bag.

"Aah, screw him anyhow," Steve said. "Zamir, you up for some freestyling?"

"For sure. I'll just swing by my place and pick up my ball. You're going to like it; it has a good grip." Zamir was proud owner of a sweet Adidas Finale of the type favored by freestyling champs. Me, I couldn't do anything with a soccer ball except maybe a wild clearance kick, so I bowed out and scooted.

I shot Zamir a raised eyebrow as we said our good-byes.

"So maybe that hairy wolf can change his habits after all."

Zamir laughed. "My father always says that proverbs are — how do you say in English? — bullshit. Maybe he's right."

* * *

Everything was settling into place, it seemed, but for me one crucial issue remained unresolved. The thing I'd been putting off, fearfully, for weeks. But what the hell. I was still so pumped after seeing Marco vanquished that I swallowed hard and decided to go for it. *Non aveva paura di niente.*

That afternoon the Manhattan Fencing Center was holding a juniors tournament at their midtown facility. Esther would be there, I was sure. From the web I'd discovered that the sports floor was hidden away in a 1920s commercial high-rise in the Garment District — not the most likely place for measuring swords, but a blessedly easy subway ride from JH.

There wasn't much space for spectators inside, so I just sidled in, leaned back against the cinderblock wall, and took in the scene. It was surprisingly bright and airy, given the general grunginess of the building. The long rectangular strips where the fencers would face off were laid out on what looked like a basketball court, and wires led out from a scoring machine on the short side of every strip. These would be hooked up to the competitors to register hits. I hadn't realized that the ancient art of swordsmanship was now completely reliant on electronic gizmos.

I spotted Esther as she emerged from the locker room. In her fencing whites she looked trim, sexy, and intimidating as hell. She was wearing a futuristic mask that resembled Daft Punk headgear; wired up to the scoring system she was Queen of the Cyborgs. I couldn't see her face, of course, but I recognized her majestic, powerful stance from jump. The girl was a shape-shifter. I'd seen her in dollar-store ghetto sweats, exquisitely silky evening attire, and now scifi battle drag. Every time she carried it off with perfect poise. I gulped: I was probably nuts to think I had any chance to get next to this Ninja goddess.

When the competition started, it was unbelievably fast — completely unlike the movies, where dueling heroes and villains prance across the soundstage in lengthy sequences, clinching, upending furniture, and somehow finding the time to snarl "have at thee, varlet!" between thrusts. In real fencing each point lasts a couple of seconds, and the action is so quick that you'd have no idea who won without checking the lights hooked up to the electronic scoring system. The movement of the blades was too fast to follow, so I focused on the competitor's bodies (*shut up*) as they skipped nimbly to and fro in what looked like an elaborately choreographed dance routine.

Esther dominated. She'd learned to grind out a decent chess game with the club's help, but in the fencing arena, as with her music, she was a stone-cold natural. I didn't have the expertise to understand what she was doing that set her apart, but there was no way to miss her panther-like grace and quickness. The scoreboard flashed as she efficiently posterized a series of hapless opponents. By the end, she'd finished first in foil and épée, took a close second in sabre, and captured the overall honors. Monstrous trophy awarded to Esther Toussaint; game over, fork inserted, done.

I slipped out and waited for her on the street in front of the building, feeling like an autograph hound lurking outside the stage door. Got more and more nervous as the minutes passed. At last she showed, in sweats with a sinister-looking weapon bag slung over her shoulder. I essayed an elaborate bow that I'd seen in the movies.

"Please accept my congratulations, milady. The Chevalier would be proud."

Her eyes narrowed. "I thought I spotted you in the corner, Mose. Would you care to tell me what you're doing here? You stalking me?"

"Nothing like that. I just wanted to see what this fencing thing is all about. And hey, um, I was kinda wondering … ." I froze, realized I was close to babbling. That wouldn't do. Reset. Pulled myself together and attempted the long three. "I thought I would ask you: Could we maybe, like, hang out together some time?"

Esther raised an eyebrow and shot me a penetrating stare. I wouldn't call it a cold stare, but it wasn't bubbling over with warmth either.

"Moses Middleton: Unless I'm sorely mistaken, I do believe you are asking me for a date. Am I wrong?"

Was I about to be humiliated? Giving myself an out — finding a way to save face — was always in the back of my own mind. But it suddenly occurred to me that Esther, too, might be wary of getting pranked. Maybe she was worried that I was the kind of guy who'd draw her in, then snicker and say "psyche!" She wanted some clarity, and fast.

"No, no, that's exactly what I'm doing," I blurted. There was no going back now. "So —" Deep breath. "Wanna go out with me?"

There was a pause, seemingly endless, as Esther considered the invitation; I thought I could see a series of emotions — doubt? pride? suspicion? — reflected in her face. I dared to push it a little further.

"You pierce my soul," I said. "I am half agony, half hope." I'd once again scoured the internet for an Austen quote, partly so I could try to brush the whole thing off as a joke if she said no. But then she flashed a new kind of smile, one that I could almost call tender, and suddenly I knew I was in.

"It is not in me to inflict agony on you, Moses," she replied in elegant Britspeak. "Since you went to the trouble to retrieve some apposite words of the great Austen, the least I can do is accept."

"Kickass!" I almost shouted, totally blowing my decorous demeanor.

"Hold a moment, young gentleman. There are conditions."

Uh-oh. I held my breath.

"Suffice it to say you will not be taking me to a superhero movie and a Taco Bell. Here are the terms: You will secure tickets to the Philharmonic. Good ones. And you will be treating me to a sit-down restaurant. Doesn't need to be schmancy; it can be affordable so long as it's nice. And quiet."

I fingered the change in my pocket involuntarily as I considered how I might summon up the requisite cheese. I could manage it, I was sure, even if it meant begging a sizeable advance on my meager allowance.

"Done," I said.

"There's more, my eager swain. You *will* be dressing for the symphony. That means jacket and tie at a minimum. A decent suit would be even better. Something classic. And no tags visible, please."

She had in mind the well-known moving-up ceremony scam. At my Middle School graduation, most of the boys showed up wearing suits with the tags still attached to the sleeves. This was so the clothing could be returned to the store for a refund afterwards. In my neighborhood nobody was going to lay out a wad of cash for a suit that was only going to be worn once before it was outgrown. Me, I could probably bum an acceptable sport coat from Julian, who wasn't much bigger than I was, or from Dad, who had some ancient jackets in the closet that might fit me with a little tailoring. So I figured I was okay in the sartorial department.

"I'm your man."

"Leather shoes?"

"Check."

"Then we seem to be in agreement. Text me the deets. I'm heading uptown to meet my mom. You, supposing you know what's good for you, will get the hell out of here before I change my mind."

She turned and strode briskly down the street. I somehow resisted the urge to gawk, knowing she'd catch me and figure I was no better than one of those street-corner butt gogglers.

I practically floated toward the subway entrance. This weird weightless feeling, I assumed, was what they meant by "walking on air." I wondered what other cornball clichés about romance — all that mushy stuff that I'd always dismissed as greeting card drivel — might turn out to be literally true, or at least meaningful. But just as I was getting all fluttery inside, a stern internal voice prompted me: Stand down, Middleton: Do not go full emo just because you're going on your first date. Too true. Had to keep it together or I'd blow this chance for sure. Still, I was definitely entering an intriguing new head space, simultaneously trippy and powered up. I liked the feeling. The days ahead were going to be very interesting indeed.

I was still rolling high when I reached the hood. As I passed through Travers Park, I happened to catch a glimpse of Steve and Zamir freestyling together. They were slapping two-ballers and looking pretty slick; evidently Steve was an apt pupil.

Sure, it was just a blacktop playground in northern Queens, but to my eyes it was a beautiful sight. Their lengthening shadows danced in harmony as the sun sank behind the distant spires of Manhattan. Just like the rest of us, they were working it together and keeping those balls in the air.

AUTHOR'S NOTE

The characters in this book hold strong opinions and express them forcefully. Readers may disagree, and that's okay. We don't all need to think alike, and we can still respect and like one another even when our views conflict.

The book proposes an interpretation of the "secret" of Soviet chess that is based on research but far from definitive. It's an ongoing debate in the world of chess that may never reach a satisfactory conclusion, especially since retrospective views of the USSR are so polarized.

I hope that anybody who has experienced New York City's admirable Chess in the Schools program and its associated events will recognize the vibe and the milieu, though I have taken liberties with the systems for scoring and pairings. With the exception of 722 and Galton, the schools mentioned are real, while the players and coaches are imaginary. (Apologies to the real-life coach at Hillcrest, if there is one: He or she is doubtless a very nice person.) The locations, too, are pretty much as described, although the neighborhood is changing so quickly that I can't promise everything will stay the same in future.

The blindfold game between Viktor and P.D. is based on Paul Morphy vs. Charles Le Carpentier (1849). Google it; it's a thing of beauty. As of this writing, Alexander Kotov's *The Soviet Chess School* is indeed available online as a downloadable PDF, though in fairness to the author it would be best to buy a copy. Young players will find it fascinating and rewarding.

Needless to say, sexual harassment and abuse are real and extremely serious problems. If you or someone you know is a victim, report the situation to a trusted adult or to child protection services.

I hope you liked Moses Middleton and crew. I'm working on the second book; any and all feedback is welcome. Feel free to let me know what you think of the characters, and where you would like the series to take them. Email me at: 722chessclub@gmail.com

CPSIA information can be obtained
at www.ICGtesting.com
Printed in the USA
LVHW022153260822
726880LV00005B/286

9 798494 351074